Inside Kasrilevke

Inside Kasrilevke

SHOLOM ALEICHEM

DRAWINGS BY BEN SHAHN

SCHOCKEN BOOKS • NEW YORK

SECOND PRINTING, 1973

Copyright © *1948, 1965 by Schocken Books Inc.*

This book contains the stories Dos Naye Kasrilevke, Kasrilevke Nis-**rofim,** Kasrilevke Moshav Z'kenim, *translated from the Yiddish by Isidore Goldstick.*

Library of Congress Catalog Card No. 65-14829

Manufactured in the United States of America

CONTENTS

CONTENTS

Author's Foreword

Of recent years all sorts of books about cities and lands and similar useful subjects have made their appearance in other languages. So I've said to myself, We imitate other peoples in everything: they print newspapers—so do we; they have Christmas trees—so have we; they celebrate New Year's—so do we. Now, they publish guidebooks to their important cities (they have "A Guide to St. Petersburg," "A Guide to Moscow," "A Guide to Berlin," "A Guide to Paris," and so on)—why shouldn't we get out "A Guide to Kasrilevke"?

Moreover, it has occurred to me, who am a native of the place and have only recently returned from a visit to my parents' graves there—it has occurred to me that there is no better way of showing my gratitude to my friends in Kasrilevke for their hospitality than by spreading the fame of their city far and wide.

In conceiving this project I have, of course, been

swayed more by considerations of public service than by personal motives. My book will serve as a guide to strangers visiting Kasrilevke. It will tell them where to get off the train; what transportation to use; where to get a tasty meal or good glass of wine; or where to enjoy an amusing play and other such wholesome fun of which there is much in Kasrilevke. For Kasrilevke is no longer the town it used to be. The great progress of the world has made inroads into Kasrilevke and turned it topsy-turvy. It has become a different place.

A GUIDE TO

KASRILEVKE

1 *Transportation*

I arrived in Kasrilevke by train. (There are trains
going there now, thank goodness!) It was autumn,
early in the morning, before prayer time. A fine
drizzle was forming puddles of thin mud. At the station I was set upon by a horde of hotel porters with
yellow whiskers, yellow coats, and bits of yellow tin
stuck on their yellow, threadbare caps.

"Mister! Grand Hotel!"

"Hotel Francia, mister!"

"Hey, mister, Portugalia!"

"Mister! Turkalia!"

Having run the gauntlet of this mob of flunkeys, I
ran into another gang of coachmen with high boots
and long whips. They all but tore me to pieces. One
of them, a strapping fellow, forcibly pulled my valise
out of my hand. I raised a howl: "My manuscripts!
my papers!" Then two other coachmen took my
part, each trying to grab me for himself. During the
scuffle that ensued I snatched my valise and slipped
away from them. I made straight for the tramway.

"This way, friends! Five kopecks a ride! Five kopecks apiece! From here to the end of Belefilir street
—just five kopecks! Five kopecks apiece!"

That was the conductor himself—a short, youngish man with a little yellow beard, a purse slung from his neck, and a button on his cap—shouting in a guttural voice. Beside him stood another man, a fellow in a long ragged coat and with a whip in his hand —the driver of the tramway. Both of them were pointing to a sort of tumbledown hut with shattered panes and standing somewhat askew. That was the "tram." Hitched to its long shafts was a lean, little white horse, chin down and dozing.

"Go easy there," the conductor called to me. "Don't get your foot caught; there's a board missing in the floor. The tramway is under repair."

I sat down cautiously in the car, put down my valise and waited. It was chilly. I kept knocking my feet together to stay warm.

"Conductor," I turned to the young man, "are we ever going to start?"

"I hope so, God willing," he replied.

"Let's have some tabacky, Yossel," the conductor was addressed by the driver, the fellow with the whip and tattered coat.

"It won't kill you to smoke some tumblings, Reb Kasriel," the conductor cut him short. "Good tobacco is liable to give you a headache."

"Never mind your wisecracks; better hand over that tabacky," Kasriel the driver insisted.

Conductor and driver each rolled a cigarette.

"When do we start?" I asked the conductor again.

"Today," he replied calmly, giving the driver a light.

I had no choice but to wait until the passengers straggled in. The first one to get on was a Jewish man in a tattered winter coat, the fur of which made it difficult to identify the species of animal it had once belonged to. It was too light for a fox and too red for a cat. The Jew in the ragged fur coat was followed by one without a coat, looking wretched and frozen. He sighed, glanced all around for a place and sat down in a corner by the door. After him a basket of apples staggered in, and hard behind it a Jewess wrapped up in three shawls, all of them in shreds. She was visibly chilled to the bone.

"Giddap! Reb Kasriel, get a move on!" yelled Yossel the conductor to Kasriel the driver, then he let out a whistle, and the tram set in motion. But it hadn't gone more than a few paces when it came to a halt. The door of the car opened and a head appeared.

"Do you happen to know if Moishe is here?"

"Which Moishe?" Yossel the conductor asked.

"A fellow with a cap," replied the head.

"Does he work in a hardware store?" Yossel inquired.

"That's right, in a hardware store," the head assented.

"I know him," the conductor rejoined, then whistled to the driver and shouted: "Giddap! Reb Kasriel, get a move on!"

We proceeded.

"Your ticket," the conductor called to me. "You don't look familiar; must be from out of town. Do you expect to stay here long? I can take you to a lodginghouse; it isn't a hotel, but it's clean and without bedbugs. And I can show you a place where you can eat cheap and you'll like the food."

I thanked him and told him that I had acquaintances in town. He wanted to know who they were, what kind of people they were and what they did for a living. I gave him a fictitious name and got rid of him. He let go of me, stepped up to the passenger in the fur coat and told him to buy a ticket. The latter shrugged his shoulders:

"What are you talking about? Why, I haven't got a groschen to my name."

"That's the third time this week you're traveling without a ticket," Conductor Yossel reminded him peevishly.

"Well, what of it? Do you expect me to walk? Or maybe you want me to rob somebody, just to please you," the fur-coated passenger replied just as peevishly.

Yossel the conductor waved his hand resignedly as he left him. He then walked up to the shivering, coatless passenger. The latter let on that he was dozing.

"See here, beg pardon, your ticket."

The man, pretending that he had just been roused from his sleep, rubbed his hands together.

"Your ticket!" Conductor Yossel repeated.

"I heard you," replied the passenger, coughing into his cupped hands.

"Never mind hearing me," Conductor Yossel said to him sternly. "Begging your pardon, fork out five kopecks and here's your ticket."

"Shush!" the shivering passenger came back. "What are you getting so huffy about? Just look at him—you'd think he was somebody!"

"Don't try to act smart," Conductor Yossel retorted. "Dish out the five kopecks."

"Tut-tut," the coatless one replied. "That's a pretty steep price. I'd think you'd bring it down a bit for me."

"I'll bring down my hard luck on your head," Conductor Yossel rejoined.

"Better hang on to it yourself," the shivering passenger countered. "I've enough of my own."

"Then I'll ask you—begging your pardon—to get off, if you don't mind." Turning to the driver, he ordered: "Reb Kasriel, halt."

Kasriel the driver stopped the tram and seemed perfectly delighted about it—to say nothing of the poor nag.

"Begging your pardon—right foot first," Conductor Yossel directed the passenger. The latter stamped his feet, rubbed his hands, and didn't budge.

"Are you waiting for a formal invitation?" Conductor Yossel asked him. "Would you like me to grab you by the collar and chuck you out in a heap? You'd better not wait till Velvel the inspector comes around (he's attending a circumcision celebration at our treasurer's just now), or you'll catch it good and proper. Reb Kasriel, giddap," he addressed the driver again, and the tram moved on.

"There's no justice in the world," the woman with the apples suddenly spoke up. "What makes this man worse than the other one, I'd like to know. Look here, you're letting the other fellow go without a ticket, aren't you? Is it because he's wearing a fur coat and this man is in rags? Are you afraid he's going to wear a hole in your precious bench, eh? Or do you suppose they'll reward you with a golden tombstone for what you're doing?"

"Who's asking you to butt in or stick up for anybody?" Conductor Yossel wanted to know. "How can you compare this fellow to the other man? Why, I *know* the other man; he comes of a good family.

Poor fellow has come down in the world. And this chap" (pointing to the chilly one) "—who the blazes knows who he is? Just a nobody, a ragamuffin!"

"Well, supposing he is a poor man, what about it?" the apple woman argued, rising. "Is that any reason for kicking him out? The idea of kicking out a man! Just imagine the terrible crime he's committed! Your nag is going uptown anyway, so what do you care if another man is sitting in the car? Supposing you did get five kopecks more, what then? Will that make your employer rich?"

"Look here, nobody is asking for your advice; you'd better come across with your own fare, and here's your ticket."

"Goodness alive!" the woman started up, slapping her skirts with her hands. "Something told me that he was going to pick on me next! Upon my word, I knew he would!"

"Well, what did you expect? Expect me to carry you for nothing?"

"What do you mean, carry me?" said the woman. "Why, the car is carrying me; you aren't. A fellow puts on a brass button and he thinks he can boss me around. See here, Mister Conductor, I can still re-member the time you worked as a helper for Leyzer Hersh, the ABC-teacher, and used to lug the little tots to school on your shoulders, with their lunch pails. So what's all this fuss about tickets-shmickets?"

Yossel didn't answer her.

"Well, what do you think of the gold mine I'm operating?" he asked me, sitting down beside me. "As you can see, that's what they're all like in this town. The people who have the money and are able to pay go on foot; and those that haven't got it and can't pay, ride on the tram. So how's a fellow to live and support an old mother and a widowed sister? See these boots?"—(pointing to them)—"You can't just ignore them either. They want to eat, too."

Suddenly there was a crash, the slamming together of two pairs of shafts, the snorting and puffing of two horses. Two coaches on the same line and going in opposite directions had run into each other. Curses flew thick:

"A plague on you! Blast you, you bloody fool! May a demon possess your father's father's father and all the generations before them to the beginning of time! . . ."

"I hope those carriage shafts choke you and shove your mouth down your throat. May the demons seek out your ancestors first; you're a more worthy son."

"What's the matter with your eyes, you hoodlum? You saw me going right, didn't you? So why couldn't you turn left?"

"And where is it written, you ugly monster, that

you must go right and I must go left? Suppose it's the other way round—I go right and you go left."

"Well, aren't you an ass? Why, that's what the two lines are for: I go this way and you go that way."

"You're an ass yourself! Where is it written that you must go this way and that I must go that way?"

Suddenly there was a grin on the other driver's face, as he said good-naturedly:

"You know what? The devil take them, their lines and all—their cars and their whole bloody tramway! Better let's have a fag, Kasriel, old dear, if you've got one. For all I care, they can go up in a blaze along with their tramway! How's your old woman these days? Is she quieting down a bit?"

"As quiet as the river Sambatyen on weekdays. The only time she shuts up is when she's asleep. And what's new with you?"

"Nothing new. They're making life pretty miserable for me. I guess I'll tell them to go to the devil."

"Don't you know what to do, you silly? Give them a piece of your mind. Tell them what's what, like me, and they'll give you anything you want."

"May the Lord give them a grievous disease, with a triple fever for good measure! What's your boor doing? Is he going into the service soon? Or isn't it time?"

"For all I care he can go straight to hell! He's afraid of a whipping and acts dumb . . . Have you got a match on you? Let's have a light."

And both drivers got into a long conversation in cabmen's lingo, like the best of friends. The two conductors likewise became involved in a very chummy chat, until Velvel the inspector came along, in a jolly mood, back from the treasurer's circumcision party and raised a row:

"Confound the both of you. So you're in a devil of a mess again, eh? Lucky for you I'm feeling pretty good after our treasurer Mottel's party. I'm telling you, boys, did he throw a party! Confound him! Must be a pretty nice job handling the money. I wouldn't mind it myself. A deuce of a lot better than being an inspector and running behind the tram like a dog. Man alive, what's up with you two anyhow? Another catastrophe, eh? Another collision, well! Can't you see where you're going? What about the passengers? Well, I don't give a hang about them! It's lucky you didn't smash the cars. Anyway, boys, you've got to disentangle those trams. Look now, Kasriel old dear, rehitch the horse to the other end and drive back to the station and Reb Azriel will follow you."

"I'd like to know why it's up to me to drive back?" Kasriel objected. "Let Azriel rehitch his

horse and let him drive back to town and I'll follow him."

"Reb Azriel," the inspector turned to him, "won't you please rehitch your horse and drive back to town."

"I should say not," Azriel replied. "It'll suit me quite all right if Kasriel rehitches his horse and goes back to the station. It won't hurt him a bit."

"I'll be hanged if I do," Kasriel shot back.

"I won't budge if it kills me," said Azriel.

"I wish it would," the apple woman spoke up, grabbed her basket and crawled out of the tram. "Wasn't that a lovely ride? And that's what they want five kopecks for! If I had walked, I would have been uptown ages ago. Whoever thought up that 'tramby' for Kasrilevke? It's a downright disgrace!"

"The only thing to do," I said to myself, "is to take to my legs and march to town."

I picked up my valise and was off on foot. A crowd of cabbies drove up behind me, whistling, shouting, and laughing:

"Well, well, so the gentleman wouldn't mix his caviar with kidney beans, eh? Just wouldn't ride with a plain coachman. Took a fancy to the 'tramby,' did you? You're lucky you escaped with your life. They might have flattened you to a pancake. Now you just climb into the wagon, mister, valise and all

—any wagon you like. We all work hand in glove—
misery in partnership. We take any affliction the
Lord may send us, as long as we all get an equal
share.— Get a move on, boys, giddap there!"

I climbed into the covered wagon and made a tri-
umphal entry into Kasrilevke.

11 *Hotels*

"If you'd like something cheap and classy, I'll take
you to a place that'll suit you just right," my coachman suggested to me, as he drove up to a two-story
building, with peeling walls bearing the large-let-
tered sign: "Hotel Turkalia." My cabman rapped at
the door with his whip handle, shouting at the top of
his voice:

"Noiach! Noiach! where the devil are you? Open
up! I've brought you a sucker."

The door opened, revealing a little man named Noiach, the doorman of the hotel. He grabbed my valise and without asking me any questions carried it up the stairs to the top story. Then he asked me:

"What kind of a room, by the way, would you like? With music or without music?"

"What music are you talking about?" I asked.

"I'm talking about the yactors. The yactors of the Yiddish te-ater are stopping here. And across the hall there's a cantor from Lithuania with twelve choir-boys. He came here for the Sabbath services. They say he isn't a bad cantor, really a first-class cantor."

"For all I know he may be a first-class cantor. But if you'll excuse me, I'd rather have a room without music."

"As you say," Noiach the doorman answered. "I can give you another room. It's entirely up to you. But if it isn't just so, don't blame me for it."

"What do you mean, 'not just so'?" I asked.

"Well," says he, "supposing you're bitten."

"Who on earth," I asked, "is going to bite me?"

"Well," he replied, "it won't be me. But there'll be those that'll bite you. We did some cleaning not long ago, just before Passover, but nothing seems to do any good, not even lamp oil."

"If that's the case," I said, "let's have the music."

Noiach the doorman showed me into a dark room,

reeking of freshly tanned leather, decayed pickles, and stale cheap tobacco. Before I had time to get my bearings, Noiach seized an object and began to slap it, as you would a soft pillow to fluff it up for somebody to sleep on comfortably. While pounding away he kept on talking, apparently to himself, and raising a savage hue and cry against somebody:

"You fathead, you jobbernowl, you mooncalf! I'll give you a sock in the puss, so your crunchers will go flying! Can you beat that?—Here's everybody coming from the train, so he flops down on the bed, boots and all, sprawls out and makes himself at home. Poor delicate boy! A fine footman you are! Why the devil didn't you open the shutters or light the samovar or shine the yactors' shoes or tidy up the cantor's room? Moishe Mordkhe, get a move on! And get the hell out of here!"

Only then did I notice a tall, strapping young fellow in high boots that were oozing with grease. So that was where the smell of leather was coming from. The footman swallowed the beating the doorman gave him without a murmur, wiped his lips unconcernedly, opened the shutters, took a look at me and burst out laughing.

"Did you ever?" the doorman turned to me. "Maybe you can tell me what's so funny about it. Seems to enjoy a couple of wallops on an empty

stomach. Moishe Mordkhe, get going!" he shouted. "Get the hell out of here! You lazy lout! Go on! You potato-gobbling, noodle-guzzling, doughnut-grabbing idiot! Go!"

Noiach the doorman then gave him a punch in the neck for good measure and kicked him out of the room.

"Quite a decent chap," the doorman then confided in me, "only a trifle lazy and a sound sleeper. You simply can't rouse him without a good trouncing! Poor fellow, works like a beast of burden. And everything he earns he gives to his sister. We had our hands full getting him to order a pair of boots.—And what'll you have with your tea? Some fresh baked-stuffs—egg cracknels, poppy-seed biscuits, or Kasrilevke frenzels?"

Noiach the doorman made a right about turn and disappeared.

"Mister, have you said your prayers yet?" somebody asked me, sticking his head into my room.

"What's that to you?" I wanted to know.

"I'd like to ask you for something," he answered.

"Who are you?" I inquired.

"A Jew," he said, "a stranger, I don't live here. I wanted to ask you to let me have your prayer shawl and phylacteries for a few minutes. Mine were stolen right here just yesterday in this first-class hotel."

The door opened again and another head, a hatless one, was thrust in and addressed me in several languages simultaneously:

"*Raznikh tovarov, pani!* Good socks! *Renkawiczki zimne,* winter gloves! *Die beste Ware* and cheap! *B'khotzi khinom*—at half the price. *Jak Boga kocham,* as I love God! Take at least half a dozen of these socks—God bless you! I didn't know who you were. There are times when you run into a Gentile nobleman and you talk to him for an hour in Yiddish; then you get it in the neck. So I've made up my mind to try Polish, Russian, and German. Thank heaven, I know several languages.—Wouldn't like a pair of good, warm gloves, would you?—Let me tell you, there was a time when I was a prosperous merchant, used to go to all the big fairs—to Yarmelinetz, Proskurov, and Poltava.—So you won't have anything else, eh? Maybe a cake of soap? Or a comb, the best there is? No? Well, thanks for what you've bought. My kids will be delighted. Say, maybe I can interest you in a good brush after all? Or a fine necktie? Or another half-dozen socks—I'll let you have them cheaper. No? You don't want to? Well, goodbye."

The man grabbed his cap and was off. Another individual stepped in; this one had his cap on.

"Buy my socks, mister, good socks and cheap!"

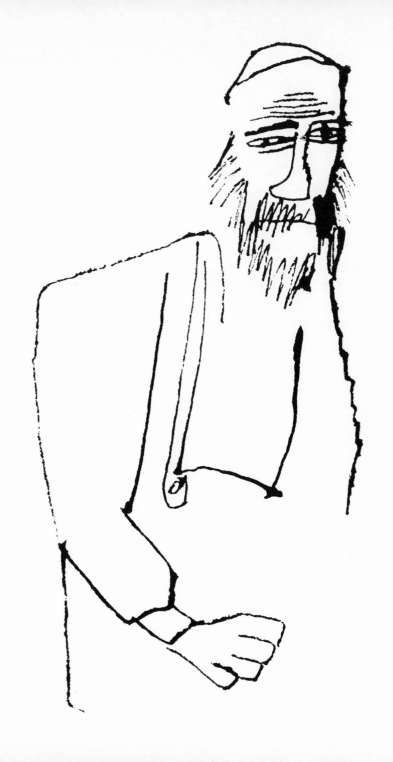

"I don't need any socks," I told him. "Thank you."

"What do you mean, you don't need any?" he protested. "Didn't you just buy half a dozen socks from the other fellow? I, too, am a poor man with a big family and I have two boys in the Russian school, you know. One boy is apprenticed to an artisan and the little tots attend the Hebrew school.—Oh, thank you, thank you! God bless you and good luck to you!"

This man was followed by another one—tall and lanky, with a frightened look on his face.

"If you want to do a good deed, as good as fasting on *tisho-b'ov*, take the rest of my stock at a bargain price. I just have a few dozen socks left."

"I don't need any socks!" I told him emphatically. "I've got plenty of socks now."

"I'll sell them to you below cost," he argued. "I won't dicker with you. Whatever you give me may the Lord return to you in good health and a long life! I have a son attending the Gymnasium; he'll be through this year. He wants to study for a doctor. 'You won't need to slave so hard, Father,' he tells me. 'I'll do the slaving then and you'll be able to rest up a bit.' That's what he tells me, my son does. In the meantime I have to help him out with a few roubles, though he's been earning some ten roubles a month himself, may no evil eye harm him.—Thank you. Keep well and good luck!"

After him came a Jewish woman, wearing a Turkish shawl and talking in a singsong:

"Are you the guest from Yehupetz?"

"Yes, well?"

"I understand you've come to Kasrilevke to buy socks. So I've brought you a few dozen as a sample. I run a sock factory. I've been manufacturing socks for ten years now."

"Whoever told you that I buy socks?" I asked her. "No, I didn't come here for socks, I don't need any socks!"

But she wasn't listening to what I was saying. She kept going, rattling on and on:

"My socks are known all over Kasrilevke. Just look at this sock! What do you think of this one?"

"But in heaven's name!" I shouted, "I don't buy any socks! I don't want any socks!"

"But you've got some socks right here," she protested.

"I've brought these socks to sell!" I shouted as I showed the woman out and locked the door, to keep out any more sock salesmen.

In less than five minutes I heard another rap at the door. "Who's there?"

"It's me!" a voice replied from the other side of the door.

"Who's 'me'?" I asked. I was afraid to open the door for fear someone might be offering me more socks.

"Dovid," came the reply.

"Dovid who?"

"Dovid Shpan."

"Who's Dovid Shpan?"

"Dovid Shpan the agent."

"What have you got?" I asked. "Maybe some socks?"

"Oh, you want some socks?" he replied. "Just wait a minute. I'll run out to the stores and bring you some!"

"No! No!" I screamed. "I don't need any socks."

I opened the door and was met by Noiach the doorman, loaded with rolls, buns, biscuits, cracknels, and frenzels.

"Whom is all this grub for?" I asked him.

"Why worry about that?" said Noiach. "You can be sure we won't throw it out. There are plenty that'll eat it. Myself, I have six munchers of my own, besides two poor orphans that I'm raising." He scowled suddenly: "Mind telling me what's the big idea? If you needed socks, why couldn't you ask me to go and get them for you, instead of Dovid Shpan?"

"Who on earth ever told him to get any socks for me?" I replied.

"I don't know who told him to," said Noiach. "I certainly didn't. That crook'll bring you socks that'll be a sight for sore eyes! Socks made in Kasrilevke!"

Just then the door opened and in walked a red-cheeked, perspiring, stocky little man, with a pipe in his mouth. Unceremoniously I took him by the arm and showed him the door:

"I don't want to be rude, but I'm fed up with your socks! I don't want any socks!"

"Good Lord!" Noiach the doorman called to me. "What are you chasing him out for? He's the proprietor of the hotel!"

"Really? Please excuse me," I said to the latter, shaking hands with him and offering him a seat. "I thought you were the man who ran out to fetch me some socks. It's outrageous! They've been showering me with socks! A deluge of socks! Please be seated."

"Thanks, I don't mind standing," the proprietor said as he sat down, puffing away at his pipe. "Where are you from, if I may ask? From Yehupetz, eh? I have an acquaintance in Yehupetz. To be exact, he's not living in Yehupetz any more. He left the place a long time ago. I wouldn't be surprised if it's eighteen years ago, and maybe all of nineteen. They say he went to Odessa. He has relations in Odessa. They have an office there; they trade in wheat—two offices, one in Odessa and the other in Nikolaev. The

Odessa office does pretty well, but the office in Nikolaev isn't doing so well, because Nikolaev has been hit, hit hard, on account of Feodosia, they say, on account of the port that's been opened in Feodosia. Feodosia has grown into a real city. I have acquaintances in Feodosia too. A fine city, Feodosia, they tell me . . ."

Seeing it was an endless story, I broke in:

"There's something I have meant to ask you," I said. "Let me see now. O yes, why do you call your place Hotel Turkalia?"

"I can still remember Feodosia as a small town," the proprietor continued. "I come from those parts myself; I'm a Bessarabian, a native of Bessarabia, a small town called Dubosara. To be exact, I was born in Belz—have you ever been in Belz? A fine town, Belz is. But how can you compare it to Kishinev?"

"He's blind in the ears," Noiach the doorman broke in, standing at some distance. "You might talk a little louder to the proprietor. His hearing apparatus is out of order. He's deaf as a fence post."

So I stepped up quite close and shouted right into his ear at the top of my voice:

"I am asking you why your hotel has such a peculiar name?"

"Why do you shout like that?" he objected. "I'm not deaf! Did you say a peculiar name? What's so peculiar about it? 'Intalia' is all right, eh? 'Portugalia' is all right too, eh? And 'Turkalia' is no good, eh? All those other names were snatched up first. So I named my hotel after the Turk.—Let me see now, what was I talking about? O yes, Kishinev. And then there are the people. I'm telling you, the people are altogether different. In Bessarabia we eat quite differently, too. In Bessarabia, when you sit down to a meal, I'm telling you, they hand you first of all that fine fish of theirs caught in their fine river. Next comes *koda*, that good fat piece of *koda*. Then they serve you on a big plate some of that beautiful, clear *mamaliga* which is cut crosswise with a long string. Next they bring on the hot, fresh *pampushkes*, pancakes, you know, and you wash them down with the genuine, pure Bessarabian wine and you follow it up with the very best *nahit* there is—that's a kind of pea . . ."

While talking he was licking his lips and, I must admit, giving me an appetite. At the same time that he was itemizing the Bessarabian dishes, there came from one direction the chanting of a Lithuanian cantor, mouthing his words tremulously, loudly, and extravagantly:

Yismeykhu bey—
malkhuskho shoi—
merey Shabbos vey—
koirey oineg! . . .

His choir was divided into two sections; while one section sang,

> *Turalirl! Turalirl!*
> *Turalirl! Turalirl!*

the other came in with,

> *Pim-pom!*
> *Pim-pom!*
> *Pim-pom!*

From another direction rose the voices of the "yactors":

> *Ti-ny-feet,*
> *Ti-ny-feet,*
> *Live-ly-and-light:*
> *Ti-ny-feet,*
> *Ti-ny-feet,*
> *Soo-thing-my-eyes.*

The footman, shining shoes behind my door, punctuated the to-and-fro motion of his brush by spitting on it at regular intervals while singing:

> *My wife has a mother,*
> *Her daughter has a man;*
> *And he beats her dear daughter*
> *With an old frying pan.*

Still another voice was heard: the voice of a woman hauling her husband over the coals. It was the proprietor's wife looking for him in all the rooms, all the while calling down on his head curious curses, most of which ended in rhymes:

"May you writhe in pain; may you shrivel and wane. May curses no end from heaven descend. A fire consume you; a plague entomb you!"

"Will you have your dinner with the proprietor and proprietress," Noiach the doorman asked me, "or in a restaurant?"

"In a restaurant," I replied. "In a restaurant!"

III *Restaurants*

KOSHER RESTAURANT
Our food is fresh and cheap
SORE INDIK, proprietress

After reading this sign, I climbed up the slippery steps to the second story of a bare-looking red-brick building. The smells that assailed my nostrils as I mounted the stairs were not especially fragrant, but an empty stomach doesn't pick and choose.

"Where can I find Sore Indik?" I inquired of an old, sallow-faced Jew sitting on the floor and busy mending an old mattress.

"A long way from here," the old man replied, slapping the mattress which gave out a greenish smoke.

"Is she gone?" I asked him.

"Gone," he answered, shaking his head. "Gone forever."

"Did she die? 'Blessed be the true Judge,' " I said and was on the point of making a getaway.

"Yes," he answered. "Six years come Passover eve. Believe me, I haven't forgotten her for a minute yet. How can you forget anyone like that? Her cooking, her baking, the way she got along with people, the way she talked to them, the way she anticipated my every whim! But what's the use of talking? Do I need to tell you? No doubt you knew her."

"How could I," I replied, "seeing that this is my very first visit to Kasrilevke."

"Don't tell me," he exclaimed. "So why are you inquiring after Sore?"

"I'm not inquiring after her at all," I answered. "I was just asking where Sore Indik's restaurant is. I saw the sign downstairs. I want something to eat."

"Something to eat?" he repeated. "Did you ever? Well, why don't you say so? Rochel! Rochel!"

A pretty, dark-complexioned young woman, with black, smiling eyes, responded to the call. Her sleeves were turned up and there were patches of flour on her hands, apron, and face.

"What's up now?" the woman asked, wiping her nose on the crease of her sleeve inside the elbow. "I don't get a chance to sieve the flour. Every minute it's: 'Rochel! Rochel!' "

"The gentleman wants something to eat," the old man said to her, continuing to slap the mattress.

"Did you say something to eat?" the woman asked in a curious singsong, as though cantillating the biblical portion of the week, shaking out her apron and fanning flour into my eyes. "What'll you have?"

"What have you got?" I replied in the same singsong.

"What would you like?" she chanted in reply.

"What would I like?" I said. "Hm—what about fish, *gefilte* fish?"

"Fish after market time?" she said. "Come now!"

"Well, make it *borsht*, then," I said, "if you haven't any fish."

"The idea, *borsht* after midday!" she retorted. "Don't you know *borsht* has to cook?"

"Everything has to cook," I said.

"I'm glad you know that much," she replied.

"Well," I said, "I don't suppose you have a pot roast either, eh?"

"Where would I get a pot roast?" she said. "We did have a pot roast, but we ate it up."

"Well," I said, "let's have some soup then."

"And what," said she, "would you like in your soup? Some manna groats, *matzos*, or soup nuts?"

"Anything at all," I told her, "so long as it's soup."

"When do you want the soup?" she asked again.

"What do you mean, when?" I said. "Right away."

"How can I give it to you right away?" she asked. "No doubt you want some chicken soup. It's no good without chicken. And if it's chicken, I first have to catch it, send it to the *schochet* to be slaughtered, pluck it, prepare it, salt it, rinse it, soak it, and put it up to cook. You'll be lucky if it's done by tonight."

"Give me anything at all then," I said, "—a bit of meat, a dish of soup, an omelet of a couple of eggs, or something salty, if you happen to have it."

"Ever see anything like it?" she asked the old man. "There isn't a thing he doesn't want.—I can get a herring if you like."

"All right then, a herring," I said; "as long as I get it right away."

"How do you like your herring?" she asked. "With an onion?"

"With an onion."

"And vinegar too-oo?"

"Vinegar too."

"And olive oil too-oo?"

"Olive oil too."

She shook out her apron again, let down her sleeves, started to go for the herring, and turned back.

"How do you like your herring—with milt or with roe?"

"Any way at all," I said, "but let's have it right away."

"Do you like smoked fish?"

"Why not?" I replied.

"What about Odessa *kefalien?*"

"I love them," I said.

"But I don't know if they've come in yet," she replied. "I don't think they're here yet, but then again maybe they are.—No, it's too early. All the same, I'll go and see, maybe they have arrived."

Rochel started and turned back.

"Are you fond of Jewish sausage?"

"I should say so," I replied. "By all means, I wish you would get some Jewish sausage. I'm very fond of sausage."

"I suppose you mean Warsaw sausage."

"Why, yes," I said, "of course, Warsaw sausage."

"In that case," she said, "you had better take a trip to Warsaw. That's where you get Warsaw sausages. In our town they sell Kasrilevke sausages, made in our own factory. But you have to have mighty strong teeth to eat our sausage. You can't possibly cut it with a knife. You might try a hatchet. The devil knows what they cram into it that makes it so hard. Not long ago they chopped up a sausage, so they found a nail in it. It would seem they put in nails to increase the weight."

"Suppose you stop talking now," the old man suggested. "Just fetch the food and let's have no more talk."

"What do you mean, just fetch the food? You've got to know what to fetch, don't you? Every man to his whim. Take yourself, for example, you like fried fish; there are others who hate fried fish and like baked fish. Then there are those of our guests who order boiled brain and eat it chopped, seasoned with onion and goose fat. And then there are some who like to eat calf's-foot jelly with dried cloves of garlic on weekdays. Then there are gluttons who'd sell their souls for derma stuffed with *farfel*. And then there are those who wouldn't—if their life depended on it—as much as touch meat seasoned with vinegar."

"Please," I said, "let me have whatever you have a mind to give me. I'm positively starved."

When Rochel left, the old man turned to me:

"She never stops talking."

"Is this your daughter?" I asked him.

"Daughter? The idea!" he replied. "Why, she's my wife, my second wife. Dear, dear, dear. Of course, she isn't like the other one. The other one— may she rest in peace—was a woman, well, you won't find the likes of her. As a matter of fact, I've nothing against this one either. Poor thing, she toils mighty hard, and she's so devoted. What a life she leads! See this wretched mattress—that's all the bedding we have. Besides I'm sick and full of whims. You have to be stronger than iron to put up with my crazy notions. To be exact, I am good-humored by nature, but if anybody ever steps on my toes, there's no telling what I might do. I let fly at a fellow's head anything I can lay my hand on. That's the kind of a hothead I am. Now, don't imagine for a minute I didn't tell her all this before we got married. I told her that living with me wouldn't be a bed of roses, that she'd be lucky to find a piece of bread in the house. Never mind meat and milk. And as for work —so I told her—she'd have to work like a horse."

"So why did she marry you?" I asked him.

"What do you mean, why?" he said to me, surprised. "Isn't the house something?"

"What house?" I asked. "Why, is this your building?"

"No," he laughed. "I mean the restaurant I'm running. It's been a going concern for years. As bad as business is just now, it's still a restaurant.—To look at Rochel, when she dresses up and goes out for a stroll, you'd think she was a countess! Why, she's a beauty—may no evil eye harm her. She's a bit faded now. You should have seen her a few years ago."

"How many children have you?" I asked him.

"O dear, O dear," he replied. "Children—that's the trouble; I have no children.—Can I offer you a drop of whisky? I've got some spirits."

"I'd like nothing better."

"I'll pour some in a dark cup," he said, pulling out of his breast pocket a flask and a small glazed cup and pouring out some spirits for me. The spirits increased my appetite even more and I felt positively famished.

Now Rochel came in with the herring. She set the dish down on the table, slapped her skirt with both her hands and exclaimed:

"I'll be blasted! I clean forgot that there is neither white bread nor brown in the house! What kind of bread do you like? Jewish white loaf or buns, or maybe rye bread?"

"Buy the first thing you see," I said. "Please, stop asking me what I like. I like everything."

"What a fussy guest you are," said Rochel. "Why,

you've got more bees in your bonnet than my husband! If my husband had his way, he'd have a fresh loaf every day. He just won't touch stale bread. Surely you can't have fresh bread daily. That's all right for a millionaire . . ."

"Get moving now," the old man said to her. "Can't you see the gentleman is starved?"

Rochel left for the bread, and a woman came in. She was lanky and had only one eye. She kept one hand in her bosom and was scratching her ear with the other.

"What'll I do, Reb Moishe Yankel? What's your advice?" she asked the old man. "My Shmulik's ear is running again . . ."

Rochel returned with the bread and began to prepare the herring for me. All the while the lanky, one-eyed woman didn't let up describing how Shmulik's ear was running. She was afraid she'd have to call in the doctor's assistant again, but she didn't know which one to go to. For no matter whom she went to, she knew in advance it was no use, because all the assistants in Kasrilevke—the devil take them—were nothing but highway robbers! Just try and give a doctor in Kasrilevke less than fifteen kopecks, he'll throw it in your face. It's not enough for the famous specialist! Did you ever? . . .

"Give a sick man a handout," a livid-faced Jew

said to me, holding out a small, shriveled hand, expressly fashioned for begging.

"Help a miserable cripple," wailed a creature walking on his hands and feet, for both his lower limbs seemed grown together and twisted under him.

"Have pity on a man with the falling sickness . . ."

I interrupted my "feast," paid my bill, and ran out of the restaurant as if pursued by a hundred demons.

IV *Liquor*

"After a dinner like this a glass of wine would be just the thing," I said to myself, as I spied a sign with a Hebrew inscription: "We sell wine, mead, and beer at low prices!"

I made my way down to a dark cellar and stepped along among barrels and casks, tubs and bottles. Off to one side I noticed a strapping young fellow with a bandaged, swollen face sitting over a trough and chopping raisins with a cleaver.

"Where is the proprietor?" I asked him.

"Did you say the proprietor?" he came back, taking a handful of raisins, smearing it across his mouth and crunching lustily. "The proprietor is busy making his special *vimorozik*."

"What do you mean by *vimorozik?*" I inquired.

"Would you like to know how *vimorozik* is made in Kasrilevke?" he asked. "You take some raisins and you keep hacking away at them. Then you dump the stuff into a big barrel, fill it up with water out of the Rotten River, and add hops. That makes it ferment, and when it ferments, it gives off a stench that simply knocks you down. So you take a few pailfuls of spirits, and dump into it a kind of powder that costs fifteen kopecks per hundredweight. Finally you strain the wine through a coarse shirt and you chalk up on the barrel: 'Vimorozik Akerman.' Now, if you want red wine, you add some gallnut to the same mixture and you write on the barrel: 'Zmir Feodosia' or 'Hungarian Malaga.' And the connoisseurs of Kasrilevke swill this concoction and smack their lips. Sh, here comes the proprietor—plague take him!" And the young man began to pound away at the raisins with all his might.

"What would you like?" said the proprietor, approaching me. He was rather short, had red hair, a hoarse voice, and one wide-open eye, which probably stayed open even when he slept.

"A glass of wine," I said.

"Wine by the glass?" he asked me, drilling his ear and looking up to the ceiling.

"Wine by the glass," I assented.

"So why did you come down to the cellar? Why didn't you go upstairs? Climb up, please, and turn right."

I climbed up, turned right, and stepped into a dark, dirty, smoky room. There were a few sickly, rickety chairs, and men sitting around, smoking cigarettes and drinking *vimorozik*. They weren't singing, shouting, pounding on the table or committing any other improprieties. They were just sitting, sipping or swilling their *vimorozik*, lighting cigarettes, sighing, moaning, and talking in an undertone.

There were two Jews sitting at a small table, heads bowed. It was easy to see that they had run out of talk. One of them spoke up:

"What do you think of this *vimorozik*, eh?"

"What do you expect?" the other replied, as though suddenly roused from his sleep. "Why, this *vimorozik* is a drink fit for a king. You just can't beat it!"

"Must ask him if he'll have some of this here kind of *vimorozik* for the Passover."

"So, you're worrying about Passover now, eh? I suppose you haven't another care in the world. The only thing you're short of is Passover *vimorozik*."

"What else, mind telling me?—O dear! What an awful fix I'm in."

"You're in one awful fix all right, when you have to sit here all day long, hiding away from your wife, so she won't pester you for money for the Sabbath."

"Don't remind me of my wife. I'd rather you fired a pistol into my heart. What can I give her? All I can give her is my misery. What an awful fix I'm in!"

"Do you suppose I'm any better off? I'm in pretty deep water myself."

"I know that you're no better off either. We're both in a fine pickle. Here's to you! *L'khayim!*"

Another couple was sitting at another table, one wearing a good coat, the other a tattered one. The owner of the good coat did all the talking, while he of the tattered looked him straight in the eyes, nodding approvingly.

"Now do you understand how Leyvi Yitskhok turns a deal to his advantage? Leyvi Yitskhok can twist and turn things and get himself and others so balled up that nobody knows where he is at. But you just leave it to Leyvi Yitskhok—he'll get out of the mess all right. I want you to know that before I tackle a business deal, I first smell it out; I take my time —no hurry. And when I know exactly what it smells like, I do a bit of fumbling all around it—this and that, noodle and attic and onion, here and there and everywhere. I figure, maybe this and maybe that— just as I'm telling you. You've simply got to think of everything. Mind you, I believe in grabbing while the grabbing is good. All the same, when the other fellow isn't looking, if I happen to notice that the whole thing is a mess, just a hopeless tangle—I simply step aside and mum's the word! They'll just have to get along without me! If the thing is fated to come off all right, it will. And if I have to do some more fumbling, well and good. Don't forget there's a place called St. Petersburg, and I know a door or two in that town. Just leave it to me, I know what's what and the right kind of lingo too. And if I want some-body to push a quill for me, I can find those that'll do it all right. The main thing is not to make any noise about it. Mum's the word!" he concluded as he bit his own fist and became silent.

Another circle of men, wearing a variety of jackets and coats and all sorts of caps, was sitting around a table and talking all together, so that their words were fused and resulted in an odd medley of topics— business, politics, *vimorozik*, old times, the younger generation, doctors, the tramway, the community taxes, the-devil-take-the-magnates-of-Kasrilevke, and so on. It's impossible to put it all down on paper. Standing off to one side was a group of perfect strangers who weren't drinking at all. They had just dropped in to hear what people were talking about and to warm up a bit while they were at it.

There was another company sitting around a table, drinking *vimorozik* and intoning a song that was a cross between Ukrainian and Hebrew. They chanted it softly and in a doleful tone, as though reciting the Penitential Prayers or the Psalms:

> *Beloved Abraham, O hark!*
> *O hear us, beloved patriarch!*
> *Why don't you intercede,*
> *Tell God of our need?*
> *O pray with bended knee,*
> *That He may set us free!*
> *Then we will once more dwell*
> *Upon the soil of Israel!* . . .

At the word "pray" their voices softened, they bowed their heads, and lifted up their hands in the manner of a devout cantor—if you will excuse the comparison—leading the congregation in prayer on the High Holy Days. The word "free," however, was uttered uproariously, furiously—*fortissimo*. At the mention of "the soil of Israel" they actually burst into tears, like little children.

"Just fancy," said one of the group, a man whose cap now covered only half of his head, eyes drowsy, and whose tongue was getting a bit tangled up in his teeth. "What would happen if, supposing, for example, they gave us back the Land of Israel, eh? Eh, Yankel? What do you say, Yankel? You're a good singer, you should know."

"The Land of Israel?" said Yankel, stretching his neck and scratching under his collar. "Did you say the Land of Israel? Well, that certainly wouldn't be bad. I understand they're doing something about it— what do you call them?—those, those . . ."

"The Zionists?" somebody helped him along. "Nonsense! Nothing will come of it!"

"Why not? There must be something to it."

"Is that so? I know what I'm talking about. I hate to talk just for the sake of talking. You know me, when I tell you a thing, I know what's what."

"You're fools, all of you!" spoke up a sickly-looking little man in a lustrine coat, talking deliberately as though counting his words, now and again putting his finger on his nose, twisting his mouth to one side and smiling contentedly to himself, his cheeks glowing. "Fatheads, that's what you are, as I'm a Jew. Just a bunch of loons! I've been looking on, keeping quiet and listening to your jabber: Zionists-shmionists; that's so much fiddle-faddle! It's easy to see you don't know chalk from cheese! If you like, *I'll* tell you what's at the bottom of it. It's like this—but you'll have to put your mind on it . . ."

He put the tip of his little beard in his mouth, closed his eyes and was deep in thought for a long while. Then, as if roused from his sleep, he beckoned to the proprietor, snapping his fingers:

"Mister—begging your pardon—will you send for another bottle of *vimorozik?*"

v *Theater*

On leaving the wine shop, I noticed a poster bearing
the following inscription in Yiddish:

 First Time in Kasrilevke!

SEE THIS YIDDISH PLAY!
The one and only ADLER FROM AMERICA!

*The Greatest Comedian
in the World!*

**You'll DIE laughing—never before such a
 BOBBE YAKHNE the shrew!
Our HOTZMAKH the clown has no equal**

Today a brand new opera!

CALEDONIA

**Don't miss this if you have to pawn your silverware!
You don't dare stay at home! Don't pass this up!
Run to the box office! Buy your tickets now!**

Hurry!   *Hurry!*

The poster bore the signature of the actor-manager-director Adler, none other than the one and only Adler from America, the greatest comedian in the world.

"Do you happen to know where the Yiddish theater is?" I asked a Jew hastening past me with a bundle of wares under his arm.

"The Yiddish what?" inquired the passer-by, coming to a halt and taking me in from head to foot.

"The Yiddish theater," I said.

"What theater?" he asked.

"Where they're giving a Yiddish play."

"Who's giving it?"

"Adler," I said. "Adler is playing."

"What Adler?"

"Adler, the one and only Adler."

"Where is he from?" he asked.

"From America."

"From America?" he repeated. "So what's he doing here?"

"He's playing in the Yiddish theater."

"What's he playing?"

"Caledonia," I informed him, "that's what he's playing."

"Goldunye," he came back, "what's that?"

I tried to get away, but he wouldn't let go of me. He wanted me to tell him what sort of thing the

"thee-ater" was, the meaning of "Goldunye," and who this Adler from America was. I explained and made it clear as I could what the "theater" is, and what "Caledonia" is, and who Adler is. He listened to me attentively, then bent over, spat, and walked off abruptly, without saying goodbye.

"Khane Beyle, whe-ah-ah you wunning to?" a young woman yelled to another all over the street, pronouncing her *r*'s and *l*'s like *w*'s.

"I'm wunning to the pway," the other replied. "Wouldn't you wike to have a wook, too?"

"I wish my mistwess would wook death in the face!" the first rejoined. "What do you think of our 'wistocwatic' wadies of Kaswiwevke, eh? She wants me to do the geese fuh huh today—may somebody do huh to death! And she wants the fat wenduhed—may she be wenduhed, wawd of the uniwuth! Ewewybody's going to the theatuh and I'm tied down. May she be tied down hand and foot, deah God!"

"Why do you wisten to youh gwand wady?" said the other. "Fuh yaw money, you can go whe'ewuh you wike."

"That's wight. I don't gib a wap what she says," the first one assented. "I'll wun home, change, and be off to the theatuh. She can hollah as much as she wikes."

The two young woman separated. I had somebody

to lead me to the theater now. My guide kept looking back and noticed that I was following her. She halted for a moment and turned right. I turned right, too. Then she turned left, and I went in the same direction. She slackened her pace; so did I. Suddenly she was off at a clip, running as if for dear life.

"What's the matter?" somebody asked her. "God be with you, what are you running for?"

"Some cwazy woon," she said pointing to me. "He's been cwose behind me for an houh now, fowowing me wight and weft. I don't know who he is."

In no time we were the center of a circle of men, women, and children. They began to point their fingers at me. A coachman drove past, I jumped into the vehicle and ordered him to take me to the theater.

In front of the theater I found a crowd of young men and girls talking, laughing, and wise-cracking.

"Let the high-born gentleman pass!" somebody shouted.

"Go easy there, you might crease his hat, heaven forbid!" another one yelled.

With much ado I managed to push through the crowd to the tiny window of the box-office. Jostled and squeezed on all sides, I inquired about a ticket.

"What price ticket do you want?" I was asked by the cashier, a long-necked, skinny young man.

"What tickets have you got?"

"We have tickets at fifteen, thirty, and forty-five kopecks."

"Haven't you anything more expensive?" I asked him in the midst of the noisy chatter and hubbub of the crowd.

At my question, the cashier jumped up from his seat, stuck his head out of the window and bellowed right into my face at the noisy band:

"The devil take the lot of you! Aren't you ever going to scatter? Look here, in another minute I'll send out Reb Lozer the policeman with a water hose! Come here," he turned to me, "step inside the gate."

The people moved aside a bit and I forced my way through the gate into a yard. There I saw a large stable or shed, with light showing through the chinks between the boards; a lot of noise came from inside it. The door of the building stood ajar, guarded by two strapping young men, who were there to make sure that no one got through without a ticket.

"Hey, walk single file there!" shouted a Jew, whose whiskers looked as if they had been plucked in spots, and with a sword dangling at his side—evidently Reb Lozer the policeman. But no one listened to him. They just wouldn't walk in single file. All wanted to get in first and were jamming into the entrance.

———

"Hey there, let me pass, you tin soldier with the wooden sword! Can't you see who's coming?" I heard somebody belaboring Reb Lozer while ploughing through the crowd, at the same time hauling the actors over the coals:

"Mummer," "ragamuffin," "starveling," "sourpuss."

I turned around to see the speaker, who sounded familiar. I looked sharply and recognized him. It was Noiach the doorman of Hotel Turkalia. He was followed by a host of women, boys and girls.

"Who is this young woman?" one of the actors asked him.

"Why, that's my wife," the doorman replied. "Don't you know my Sore Perl? And these are my children."

"And this."

"That's my mother-in-law."

"And this one?"

"That's a sister of my wife."

"And who is the young man?"

"That's her bridegroom."

"And who is the girl?"

"That's the bridegroom's sister."

"And who is this boy?"

"That's the bridegroom's sister's bridegroom."

"And who is this girl here?"

"That's his sister, that is, the bridegroom's sister's bridegroom's sister."

"That's a pretty nice family you've got, Reb Noiach!"

"Salt in your eyes and stones in your heart!" Noiach replied. "The least you could do is add, 'May no evil eye fall on them,' you ham actor, you cheap comedian, you bear-leader, you bellower, you bun gulper!"

Directly behind Noiach the doorman, the high-booted lackey of the hotel was shoving ahead. One of the two actors at the entrance gave him a wallop from behind and pushed him into the theater.

Other men and women, for the most part without tickets, were forcing their way through the door. Among them I recognized the proprietor of Hotel Turkalia with a very fat woman, moving as if on wheels and swaying like a duck.

"Oh, so you're here too," I said to the proprietor, forgetting that he was as deaf as a post.

"Not too bad," he replied, shouting at the top of his voice, as if I were the one who was deaf. "They don't sing too badly."

"Is this your first time here?" I asked him.

"This is Reb Lippe's stable," he rejoined. "All year round they keep cows or horses here."

"Get a move on there," the fat woman called to

him, tugging him by his coattail. They walked on and took seats in the front row.

"Listen here, you actors! Where are you, anyway?" a lady wearing a hat with a white feather and brilliants, spoke up. She was flanked by a dandy with a bowler and trimmed whiskers.

One of the actors jumped forward, a lanky fellow with a short coat, a dirty shirt, and a hungry-looking face.

"What can I do for you, madam?"

"What do you mean, do for me?" she replied. "We bought tickets, don't you know? Why aren't they showing us to our seats?"

The lanky fellow with the hungry face took their tickets, led them to the front and was about to show them to their seats—they were taken.

"Excuse me, these aren't your seats," the actor said to a boy and a girl comfortably seated and cracking nuts out of a paper bag.

"Who told you these weren't our seats?" the young man shot back without interrupting his nut-cracking operation.

"Show me your tickets," the actor said to them, taking their tickets and pointing to where they should be sitting, much lower down.

"What do you mean, ordering us where to sit?" the young man objected. "What's this anyway—a house of worship, a synagogue?"

The actor got into a long argument with him. The boy and the girl, however, didn't budge, or stop cracking nuts. The lanky actor with the hungry face tried similar persuasion with all the other spectators in the theater. The entire audience, however, was securely seated and wouldn't give up their places for anything less than the use of force.

The lady with the white feather and the brilliants grew angry:

"What kind of arrangement do you call this?"

She clamored for a refund and wanted to know where policeman Lozer was, anyway.

She didn't quiet down until two extra chairs were brought up front especially for her.

The lamps were gradually lit and gave off smoke and a strong smell of gas. One by one the musicians took their places in front of the stage which was curtained off with a sheet. The first member of the orchestra to appear was the double bass, a big man with thick earlocks and eyes looking daggers. He was followed by the kettledrummer, a hunchbacked, baldheaded young man. Then came the trumpeter, short and thick-lipped; the flutist with a tuberculoid face; a trombone player with roguish, shifty eyes; and two or three young violinists. Last of all came the first violinist, the senior instrumentalist and conductor of the orchestra—a young man with thickly pomaded red hair and wearing a white paper dicky, a big blue necktie, and a short coat. Facing the audience, he cracked each of his fingers and smiled to a white-gloved girl back in the audience.

Taking their places, the musicians set about tuning up their instruments. First the conductor tapped his violin with his bow. This was a signal for the thick-lipped trumpeter to blow a note. All the other instruments then followed, each giving out its characteristic sound, speaking its own language. The violin lamented and sobbed dolefully, the trumpet said "gobble-gobble," like an infuriated turkeycock, the double bass groaned like a bear and the flute whistled mockingly at the rest of the instruments. Together they made an uproar like hundreds of women talking together at a fair simultaneously with the quacking and gaggling of swarms of ducks and geese.

Soon a young man in a green caftan appeared on the scene, carrying in one hand a sheaf of papers and in the other—half a bun and a piece of herring. He sat down on a low stool in front of the stage and had a bite to eat.

"Who's that?" I heard the lady with the white feather ask her escort.

"That's their prompter," her beau replied.

"What do you mean, prompter?" she asked again.

"He reads to them what they have to say," he explained.

From the other side of the curtain could be heard snatches of conversation between the actors:

"Where the devil is Fradl the primadonna?"

"She went to the cobbler's. Couldn't come on the stage. Heel came off."

"It wouldn't have killed her to attend to her shoes in the daytime. What a primadonna!"

"Avreml, take off your pants!"

"What's wrong with my pants?"

"Wouldn't you make a fine shrew—in pants!"

"I'm wearing a skirt over them. So what's wrong with them?"

"I know you've got a skirt on. But what'll happen when they throw you into the fire? You're supposed to land head down and feet up. Your pants will show."

"Better give me a drag from your cigarette, you lousy scamp . . ."

"Hotzmakh, where are your whiskers? Why don't you stick 'em on now?—Rivke, smear some chalk on your face.—M'nashke, put that hump on your back; it'll make you look more like a Jew.—Where on earth are the feet?"

"What feet?"

"Did anybody fetch those feet from the butcher's?

I've told you time and again we've got to have a cow's foot when 'Caledonia' is played, haven't I? The devil take you! Velvel, what kind of a manager are you anyway, you lubber?"

Suddenly a deafening racket was started up by the audience, who had grown impatient. Then somebody ran through the crowd, ringing a bell. That quieted them somewhat. A few minutes later the shouting and stamping began again. The man with the bell ran through the crowd again. This procedure was repeated a number of times, until the redheaded fiddler jumped up, pumped his head up and down a few times, adjusted his collar and blue necktie, came down with his baton, and the musicians struck up a tune. Before long the spectators were at it again, yelling and stamping. Then the orchestra played another number. The noise did not, however, subside altogether until the sheet rose and the play began.

The first to come on the stage was a girl in a petticoat and disheveled hair, looking as if somebody had just slapped her face soundly. She intoned a mournful song about a poor orphan girl to the tune of the Russian song, "Stands a Lofty Mountain, Lofty Mountain"—"Stands an orphan, an orphan . . ." The audience joined in: "A poor little orphan, a poor little orphan," at first softly, then louder and louder, until the actress' voice was completely drowned out.

Then one of the actors bounded out on the stage and appealed to the spectators, "Quiet, please!" They complied at first, but not for long. Soon they were at it again, the entire audience supporting the singer: "A poor little orphan, a poor little orphan . . ."

The same actor leaped forward again and again, until he lost patience and bawled angrily:

"Aren't you ever going to shut up? In another minute I'll call Reb Lozer the policeman with the hose. He'll soon tell you where to get off."

The audience stopped singing, and began expressing various opinions about the performer. Somebody suggested that she sounded like a "folding bed"; another, that it would be a good deed to hand her a bun. Those in the rear seats shouted for silence. It didn't help. Not until the clown dashed out on the stage, a man with a curious fur hat on his head, whiskers on one side of his face, earlocks reaching almost to his belt, shoes and long stockings. He was squint-eyed and hunchbacked. Carrying a basket of wares, he ran up and down and across the stage like mad, enumerating the goods he had for sale:

"Whips and strips! Matches and latches! Paper socks and crystal smocks! Cloaks and yokes! Buy, dear womenfolks!"

Every now and then he would tug at his earlocks, jump, and let out a cry:

"Hotzmakh! The devil take me!"

The audience simply went wild over him; he brought down the house; there was tumultuous and continuous applause for a half hour, shouts of "Hurrah, Hotzmakh!" and the pounding of canes against the seats. They just wouldn't stop. The clown tried to silence the audience with energetic gestures of his hands. That whipped them up to still greater ecstasy, and the shouts grew even louder:

"Hotzmakh, let's have a jig, Hotzmakh! Hotzmakh!" Then suddenly . . .

Suddenly there was a flapping of wings overhead, something shot down and landed squarely on the hat with the white feather belonging to the lady with the brilliants. The lady nearly passed out with fright. A hue and cry was raised in the theater: "Help! Help! . . ." Then somebody yelled, "Fire!" That was the last straw. People made a wild scramble for the door, jumping over the heads of other spectators. There were shouts:

"Khassy, where are you?"

"Yankel, this way!"

"Rivke, bear up!"

"Mottel, I'm dying!"

"Brokhe, don't yell!"

"Benny, where is Yentel?"

"Mama, here I am, Mama . . ."

Another minute and we would have been done for. Luckily Noiach, the doorman of my hotel, had an idea and saved us all from being trampled to death. He jumped up on a chair, shrieking at the top of his voice:

"Fools! Blithering idiots! Blinking simpletons! Bullcalves! Doughheads! Panic mongers! Milksops! What's all this rumpus about? What are you squawking for? Where are you dashing to? In a minute you'll be flattened out like pancakes! Ninnies, what's frightened you? A silly bird? Can't you see, a bird just jumped off its perch. Reb Lozer, why don't you do something? Put the hose on! Fiddlers—a plague on you!—give us something jolly, toderi-deriraderideradaride!"

The musicians struck up a lively tune, and the crowd started to settle back in their seats. I stole carefully out of the theater, jumped into a cab and asked the driver to take me to Hotel Turkalia. The vehicle bumped me over the cobbles, halted now and then and bounced on again.

"Why do you stop every little while?" I asked the driver.

"The devil knows," he replied.—"Giddap there! —Somebody got the brilliant idea to light up the mud puddles of Kasrilevke; so they thought up a kind of lighting system—these crazy 'lanters.' It's just impossible to drive now, because the horses shy at the posts. Our horses aren't used to lighting.—Giddap!—Every now and then they devise some fresh nuisance: first it was the bloody 'tramby'—a plague on it!—Giddap!—Then these damned 'lanters' to frighten the horses with. And now there's a rumor, they're going to condemn the water from the Rotten River.—Giddap!—But, let me tell you, they're dashing their heads against a stone wall, because the water carriers say they wouldn't, for the life of them, let Kasrilevke drink well water.—Giddap!—Those moneybags don't know what to think up next. They can all go to blazes! People say that all these newfangled notions come all the way from Yehupetz. It would seem that the 'ristocrats of Yehupetz haven't a thing in the world to worry about.—Giddap!—So they sit around and rack their brains how to rob people of their livings, grab the last morsel of bread out of a poor man's mouth. The pestilence take them in Yehupetz!—Giddap, there, giddap! . . ."

Fires

At Hotel Turkalia, I waged war all night with wild animals that set upon me and took revenge on me for not wanting to sleep with them and making my bed on the sofa.

"What good will it do you?" they taunted me. "We're going to bite you anyway and, what's more, you'll find the sofa pretty hard on your head. You'll get off it all broken up."

Suddenly I heard an alarm bell: clang, clang, clang! This was immediately followed by a hubbub made by people running and shouting, "Fire, fire!" I jumped up and ran to the window. Half of the sky was red, as red as fire, the other half was black. Half of the town was strangely illuminated, the other half was steeped in pitch darkness.

I threw on my clothes and ran out into the street. A strange shouting came up from the distance, a wordless din. At the same time people were trudging sleepily in the direction of the fire, shuffling along, yawning, shivering with the cold, and telling each other tales of miraculous experiences: who was the first to hear the alarm and how they happened to hear it. They were each speculating differently about whose house was on fire. Somebody said: "It's Yossel's house." Another person suggested: "It's Menashe's house." A third one insisted: "It's neither Yossel's nor Menashe's house—it's Sore Zissel's."

"Sore Zissel my eye," another passer-by argued. "Why, Sore Zissel's house is on the Yordige, and this fire is in the old town."

"It's no more in the old town than I am in the sky," another voice replied. "Don't you see it's near the bath house?"

"Shush, what's the need of arguing?" somebody tried to pacify them. "Suppose we take a stroll over there and then we'll know exactly where it is." They moved on and I followed them, listening to their conversation. Somebody said:

"This looks like a put-up job."

"How can you tell?"

"Because the house was insured."

"How do you know it was?"

"What do you suppose? It wouldn't be burning if it wasn't insured. A house doesn't set itself on fire."

"Say, Yankel, isn't it burning beautifully? Isn't it just lovely?"

A little cottage was on fire like a Sabbath candelabrum, sticking out blood-red tongues. The roof was gone, the rafters were crackling, the windows were bursting, and a thick smoke coiled up blackly and rolled on and on over other houses, big and small. Women were wailing over the calamity that had come down upon them in the dead of night, and little tots were bawling and shivering, while trying to warm their chilly little bodies by the fire.

Here an entire household was squatting on a feather bed and a few pillows, which was all they had managed to rescue from the fire; and there a woman in the family way, with a pot and a goose-wing duster in her hand, was telling another woman how it all started:

"O my, O my, it all started from Shimmen the carpenter's house. It seems they were using—woe is me!—an oil lamp at night. There are a lot of shavings, you know, in a carpenter's shop—what a calamity! Maybe it was a match, or a cigarette; and maybe the owner himself did it—I mean G'dalye—what do I know? I wasn't there. But in the meantime —oh, it's just too terrible!—a lot of poor people have lost everything, been stripped of everything they ever had—O dear, O dear!—Come to think of it, what am I hugging this pot and duster for? I wish I knew why!"

"What a misfortune! What a blow!" a young woman was lamenting in a liturgical singsong, wringing her hands. "What'll I do now? Didn't save a straw-aw! Where's our next meal to come fro-om? Where'll I go to with my little to-ots?"

Young men were dashing about like demons, like maniacs, in and out of the burning cottage, leaping into the flames, rescuing whatever they could lay their hands on, one of them grabbing the leg of a chair, another the pendulum of a clock, still another a broom.

"Where on earth is Elye with the hose?" a member of the fire brigade shouted, looking in all directions.

"Here I am, here I am," replied Elye, a little man, fussing with a hose.

"Whatever are you doing? What are you fussing for so long?"

"I'm sewing up the hose, it split open," Elye replied.

"Where's Fishel with the pails?" screamed a dark-skinned fellow in a tattered fringed vest, with a smoke-smudged face and a hoarse voice.

"Fishel! Fishel!" all the rest joined in.

"What's all this 'Fisheling' about?" somebody spoke up, apparently none other than Fishel himself. "Did you ever? Can't think of anything better than bawling their heads off—Fishel-Fishel! Fishel-Fishel!"

"Where are those pails of yours?" somebody asked.

"The pails are here all right," Fishel rejoined. "But

what'll you do with them, when Groinem with the barrel isn't here yet?"

"Fishel, would you mind grabbing a few pailfuls of water from the neighbors in the meantime?"

"Why me?" Fishel objected. "Let Elye do it."

"Elye, grab a pail and run for some water."

"How can I? Can't you see I'm busy with the hose? Let Mottel go."

"Mottel, go and get a pail of water somewhere."

"Where do you expect me to go? I don't know a soul here. Let Anshel go."

"Anshel, say, run and fetch some water."

"Me? Why, I wouldn't know a door from a window around here. Let Dovid go."

"Hush, hush! Here comes Groinem with the barrel! He's coming! He's coming!" Everybody made a dash for Groinem's barrel, Elye with his hose in the lead.

Groinem, a man with a shining face and peeling skin, was shuffling along very calmly and deliberately, his coattails tucked into his boots. A scraggy, wizened little horse was dragging behind him, wearily pulling its hoofs out of the mud. Both Groinem and his horse looked very sleepy.

"Welcome, Reb Groinem! And here we were afraid you weren't going to show up today, heaven forbid."

"Tell me another," said Groinem. "Who else'll do

it if I don't? What do you take me for, a youngster? Why, the minute I heard the first clang, I was beside my horse. True enough, my old woman tried to stop me. 'What's the sense,' says she, 'crawling out into that mud? It's a pity on the poor animal,' says she; 'it's fagged out from the day's work.' But who'd ever listen to her? I like to do a good deed, and especially where human life is at stake—poor people burnt out. That's mighty serious!"

"Heaven grant you long life for what you're doing! We're simply dying for a bit of water. The neighbors haven't a drop."

The men of the fire brigade with their empty pails —led by Elye with the hose—began milling around the barrel.

They got busy with the pump and the pails, but the pails just wouldn't fill.

"What do you call this, Reb Groinem? Are you crazy or out of your mind? Look here, you came with an empty barrel."

"What do you mean, an empty barrel?" Groinem shot back. "I'm telling you it's full, full to the brim. How can you say a thing like that?"

"See for yourself," somebody spoke up. "Your barrel is empty, as empty as a drum."

"What are you talking about?" Groinem replied, contemplating the barrel. "What you say is Greek to

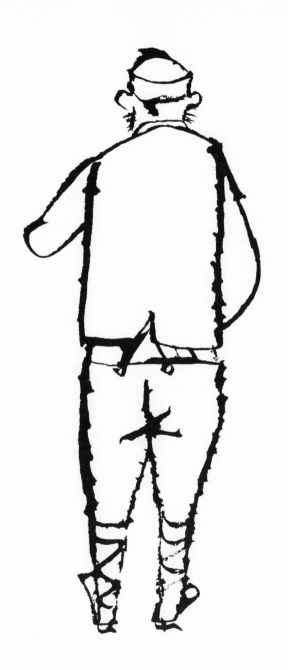

me. I can't make you out. The idea, empty! May my enemies have empty stomachs and insides!"

Groinem sounded the inside of the barrel with his knuckles. He then walked all around it until he noticed that the plug was missing.

"Yes, as I'm a Jew, an empty barrel!" He clutched his head with his hands and began calling down curses—without naming the object of his imprecations:

"The cholera seize him! A horrible and fatal disease! May his days run out! May he dry up! May he shrivel up!—When could that plug have come out? —May the earth swallow him up alive!—And where's it gone to?—May a consuming fire devour you, wretched *shlimazl* that you are!"

The last remark was addressed to the poor nag, against which Groinem now vented his bitter heart, emphasizing his words with a thrust of the whip handle against the animal's flank. The horse blinked, lowered its chin and looked aside, as if to say: "I'd like to know what I've done to deserve this whack. Socking a fellow without rhyme or reason! It's no trick, you know, to hit a horse, a dumb animal, for no cause whatever."

"May a black year descend upon you!" Groinem said under his breath. "I can see it all now. Here I kept on pouring all for nothing! Now I know what was the matter; it seems the barrel didn't have a plug in the first place. Ruin seize you this very night! May you collapse, God willing, and fall to pieces!"

"Water, water," shouted those who were doing the rescue work. "Hurry, hurry, fetch the pails! Let's have the water!"

"Did you say pails? Did you say water?" the firemen retorted. "Can't you see there isn't a drop of water?"

"What do you mean, there is no water?"

"There is no water means there just isn't any water."

"What happened to the water?"

"All the water has run out of Groinem's barrel—and there's nothing you can do about it."

Suddenly that strange clang that I had heard before was repeated: boom! boom! boom! Now the other half of the town was lit up.

"Another fire! In the new town!" several voices screamed in unison, and the spectators and the fire brigade started to run in the direction of the new town.

"Two fires in one night," Groinem said to himself, "that lets me out. I have a wife and children of my own. I don't take any pay for it. So if I feel like it, I carry water, and if I don't feel like it, I don't. My nag isn't made of iron, either. It's a pity on the dumb animal. Poor thing, it toils hard enough all day long; would you expect it to be tramping about all night too? You'd think it had nothing else to do. The community won't force me. Let them go to blazes! Come, brother," he said to his horse, "let's go home."

VII   *Bandits*

When I got back to the hotel from the fires, dawn was beginning to break. I threw open the door to my room and was flabbergasted: I saw three queer-looking men whom I had never seen before rummaging about with a candle. My bed was upset, my clothespress was open, my suitcase lay in the middle of the room, and my papers and manuscripts were scattered helter-skelter on the floor.

"What's all this? Who are you? What are you doing here?" I asked a fellow with red whiskers and a blue wart on his nose.

"Let him see your knife and he'll tremble in his boots!" one of the trio said to the red one with the blue wart.

Redbeard didn't say a word. He just locked the door, stooped down, pulled a long, sharp kitchen knife out of his high boot and waved it before my face from side to side and up and down like a magician.

"Want to know who we are? We're the town bandits!" I was informed by one of the gang, a swarthy fellow with a cataract on one eye. When he pronounced the word "bandits," his good eye glared furiously and he gritted his teeth like a murderer.

"Money! Come across!" exclaimed the third member of the group, a tall man with a hoarse voice. He grabbed hold of my lapel and shook me like a palm branch.

"Is it money you want?" I said. "Do you expect to get money from me? Where do I get money? God has spared me from it."

"You're lying!" the creature with the cataract said to me. "Better hand over all the money you've got this very minute. Else—say goodbye to everything. We're giving you two minutes to think it over and one minute to say your prayers."

To convince me that they were in dead earnest, Redbeard with the wart on his nose stepped up to me again, pumped his knife up and down and swung it to and fro, in the manner of a palm branch at the *Hallel* prayer on the Feast of Booths.

"Why do you stand there like dummies? Tie him up," the hoarse fellow said. "Where's the rope? Let's tie him."

"Why go to all this trouble?" I spoke up. "Here, take all I've got, my purse and the few roubles in it, and let me go. What do you want with me? I'm a father of children—may no evil eye harm them— four girls and two boys; the youngest isn't a month old . . ."

The three bandits talked things over among themselves in their thieves' jargon, counted the few roubles in my purse, and subjected me to the following cross-examination:

"Where are you from?"

"From Yehupetz."

"What's your name?"

"Sholom Aleichem."

Mistaking my name for the customary Yiddish greeting, they returned the compliment by saying, "Aleichem Sholom," adding, "your name, please."

"Sholom Aleichem."

"Aleichem Sholom. We're asking you what they call you."

"Sholom Aleichem—that's what they call me."

"An odd name. What do you do?"

"I'm a writer."

"We're asking you what you do, your occupation."

"I'm a writer."

"So what do you write? Petitions or documents or denunciations?"

"I write articles and story books for Jewish children."

"In other words, you're a book vendor, an author."

"An author."

"So what are you doing here?"

"I've come to see Kasrilevke."

"Is that all?"

"That's all."

"No business whatever?"

"None."

"And you've gone to some expense to come here?"

"I've gone to some expense, all right."

"What good does it do you?"

"It gives me something to write about."

"Write where?"

"In the papers."

"What papers?"

"Yiddish papers."

"Are there Yiddish papers?"

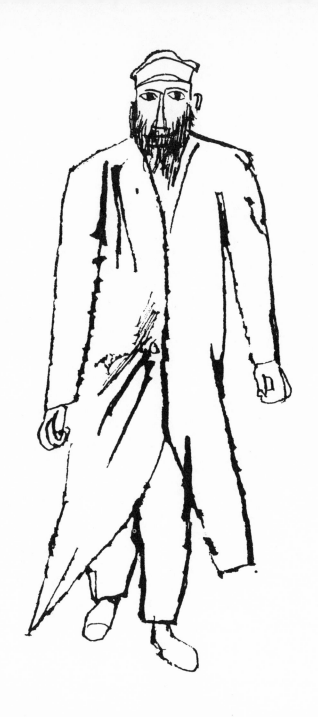

"What do you suppose?"

"What do they do with them?'

"They print them."

"Where do they print them?"

"In Warsaw."

"What are they good for?"

"For reading."

"Who reads them?"

"Jews."

"Does anybody pay you for writing?"

"Naturally."

"Now you're talking! What do you get for it? How much do you get for it? How much do you make a week?—Do you smoke? Where are your cigarettes?"

I took out my cigarette case and passed it around.

"Is this silver?" the bandit with the cataract asked me, weighing the cigarette case in his hand. "Silver or base metal?"

"As base as they make them; costs thirty kopecks," I replied, as we all lit our cigarettes.

"Where's your watch?" the one-eyed chap called to me, as he searched all my pockets. "Haven't you got a watch?"

"I do have a watch," I said, "and a good one at that, a gold one, but it's in pawn in Yehupetz."

"That's too bad," remarked the husky-voiced

thug, "we could have made good use of it just now. We need a gold watch in the worst way."

"Why do you need a gold watch so badly?" I inquired.

"A gold watch—why you can sell a gold watch," he explained, "and get good money for it."

"Confound him!" the third bandit interfered. "A poor beggar like ourselves."

"Good night," the bandits said to me as they made for the door. "Next time you leave, you had better lock the door, and don't you depend on miracles from heaven or on the honesty of the town's thieves. Excuse us if we've troubled you."

"Not at all," I rejoined. "I'm only sorry you found so little . . ." I was about to show them out when the husky-voiced bandit put his finger on his lips and drawled out in the tune of "Caledonia":

"Mum's the word—mum-m-m-m-m!"

At the same time, Redbeard with the wart whipped out his knife and waved it a few times over his head, as if to say: "If you so much as say boo, your life isn't worth a copper."

"Help! Help! Help!" I let out the weirdest shrieks when the prowlers had left, and roused the entire house. There was a wild scramble from every part of the hotel. Women jumped out of beds in their petticoats, and the menfolk—if you will pardon me—in just their drawers. They thought there was a fire.

"Another fire?"

"What's burning?"

"Where's the fire?"

"Whose house is on fire?"

"Hush, hush, nobody's house is on fire," Noiach the doorman cried out. He turned to me. "I'd like to know why you're shrieking like a lunatic calf. Why are you bawling like in a madhouse? You're liable to wake up all the yactors!"

"Robbers, murderers! Bandits have just set upon me and robbed me!"

On hearing the word "robbers," the entire crowd was horror-stricken and raised a wild rumpus, all talking at the same time.

"Robbers?"

"How many robbers?"

"Three robbers!"

"What did they look like?"

"Two young ones and an old one!"

"Did they have knives?"

"Why did you keep quiet?"

"Were you afraid to yell?"

"Robbers of all things! Heaven help us!"

"There were robbers in the other yard, too, yesterday—choking a woman—cleaned her out of everything—they found a jimmy . . ."

"Dangerous to stay alone in the house . . ."

"We'll soon have to run away from Kasrilevke."

"Robbers, can you beat that? As if it weren't enough . . ."

"Catch 'em! Catch 'em! Catch 'em!" a feminine voice was suddenly heard shrieking outside, accompanied by the scamper and racket of a lot of people. "Catch 'em! Catch 'em!"

"I've got 'em, got 'em!"

"I've got one! Got two!"

"Tie them! Got the third one too? Tie him! Tie him! . . ."

"Go easy there. Don't tie him by the head. Tie his feet, get his feet! . . ."

"Zelde, gimme your kerchief, Zelde!"

"Well, did you hear that? They've been caught!" Noiach the doorman called to us and made a dash outside with a lantern, and all of us after him.

"Well, what's doing?" Noiach shouted into the dark, in the direction from which the voices were coming. "Have you got them?"

"We've got them all right!" a feminine voice was heard out of the dark.

"Are they tied?"

"They're tied all right!"

"The three of them?"

"Every last one!"

"Well, let's at least take a look at them, see what their mugs look like," Noiach the doorman suggested, and beckoned to us to accompany him. We followed the lantern to the three nabbed robbers and found lying on the ground three fettered—turkeys!

The turkeys lowered their blue beaks, puffed through their noses, and blinked their eyes at the light of our lantern. The women, in scanty attire, told us breathlessly the story of the turkeys—how they got out of the pen, no one knew how: whether it was thieves, or whether a weasel had run past and frightened them. But thank heaven, they were caught; else the loss would have been goodness knows how great.

"Blast you, bloody fowlmongers!" Noiach exploded and called them down for all they were worth. "The demon possess your turkey-goose-duck-wing-feather-dusters! . . ."

He kept pouring forth his choice, sharp, pointed expressions. The crowd gradually scattered, yawning, everyone going back to sleep.

I stood alone in the midst of the mud, bewildered by the night and its terrors and alarms. A dank chill gripped my body and penetrated every limb. Here and there a faint light loomed in a window. Blue wreaths of smoke curled up out of a stray chimney.

A bright streak appeared above the horizon. From a number of places rose the crowing of roosters, which were tuning up their throats and vocalizing in every imaginable pitch and style: "Cock-a-doodle-doo!"

It was getting light now.

THE POOR

AND THE RICH

1 *The Delegation*

The great and beautiful Gentile city of Yehupetz, which more than a thousand years ago—back in the days of Saint Vladimir—spread out higgledy-piggledy, lengthwise and crosswise, uphill and downhill, on the bank of the venerable old Dnieper, hadn't seen in many a decade the kind of Jews that it saw on a certain morning toward the end of summer.

Now you mustn't suppose that there is a dearth of Jews in this non-Jewish town. Quite the contrary. As is well known, Yehupetz has had Jews in its midst from the days of antiquity on; and, it should be added, it craves them about as much as a man craves a headache.

For no matter when you come to Yehupetz and no matter what newspaper of theirs you pick up, the first thing that strikes your eye is the word "Jews." Thus you will read that such and such a number of them have applied for admission to the university but were not taken in; such and such a number of them were caught in a nightly raid (aimed to ferret out non-resident Jews) and *were* taken in. The reverse has never been known to happen: that Jews seeking admission to the university should be accepted and those caught in a raid should be rejected. This is about as possible as it is for a famished man to mistake another man's mouth for his own and to cram food into it by error.

But to get back to our story. What kind of Jews were those on that particular morning? They were citizens of Kasrilevke. Not just ordinary citizens either, but select men, chosen to execute a mission of the greatest importance, to perform a deed of extraordinary merit; they were the finest, the worthiest citizens of Kasrilevke, the very cream of the town. I could easily name them, but that's unnecessary, since a Jew of Kasrilevke doing a good deed doesn't seek any honor outside his home town and isn't accustomed to having his name published abroad; he is quite content with what recognition he receives on the spot. What's more, there are times when he is grateful if his townsmen at least don't haul him over the coals for his meritorious act.

Among these select men there was an older man, indeed a very old man, past eighty, stooped and leaning on an old cane as he walked, but still getting about pretty well. He wore his Sabbath best: a gay-colored, silken, sleeveless tunic over an old, threadbare, but satin gaberdine, with a fur hat on his head.

The other men in the group were not as festively

attired, but they were, nevertheless, in a festive mood, walking briskly, though with a somewhat strained and nervous gait, and carrying bags bulging with prayer shawls and phylacteries, along with umbrellas, uncommonly big umbrellas, whose purpose only heaven knew, since it was neither raining nor was the sun especially hot.

The author of this story has noted for some time that there are certain Jews who just can't be separated from their umbrellas, either summer or winter. I've seen a good many of them in my day, yet I've hardly ever seen their umbrellas held open over their heads, as one would, after all, expect them to be. Most often you meet a Jew scurrying on, bent over, with the wind lashing at his face, parting the skirts of his coat and turning them up—if you will pardon me for saying so—over his head; while his umbrella is flapping away at his calves.

On one occasion I was curious enough to stop one of these Jews, have a look at his umbrella and take hold of it in my hand. Well, I found that it weighed quite a few pounds and that it was almost impossible to open it. If you did open it, you were through with it: it just wouldn't close, at least not so easily. The ribs would be sure to stand on end and the umbrella would be converted into a kind of parachute, so that a strong gust of wind might—heaven forbid—lift you up and carry you off, along with the umbrella, away up into the clouds, almost like an airplane. But never mind the umbrellas; let's get back to the Jews.

They strode on rapidly, as if driven by someone, or as if afraid of appearing late at some celebration, banquet, or meeting. They talked at the top of their voices, all together, all the while gesticulating with their hands, as is their wont. It was only at odd times that they stopped, folded their arms and contemplated the gorgeous, towering buildings of the city; they just couldn't look their fill.

"Well, what do you think of this little cottage?" said a member of the group, pointing to a tall, magnificent structure, while shoving his cap to the back of his head, puffing like a bellows and heaving his sides like an exhausted nag. "You know what's what in cottages, don't you? Quite a cottage, eh?"

"Yes, not a bad sort of cottage," the other replied quietly and scarcely able to breathe.

"What do you figure this cottage is worth?" asked an asthmatic with a sparkle in his eyes and arms akimbo.

"This house?" spoke up a man with a high forehead, apparently an adept in figures and a connoisseur of houses. "I reckon that this little cottage along with the grounds should be worth, in this town, all of a hundred thousand."

"Ha-ha-ha." The laugh came from a young man with a pale face on which a sparse stubble was just beginning to sprout. "Did you say a hundred thousand? I only wish we all had the money it cost over and above that."

"You fool!" exclaimed the asthmatic with the sparkling eyes. "If you needs must be wishing, why not wish we had the fortunes owing on the house?"

A conversation about houses then ensued, a drawn-out conversation which served no other purpose than as a pretext for stopping. For, as a matter of fact, they were all good and tired by now from walking uphill and would have liked nothing so much as to halt awhile to catch their breath.

"No doubt you are finding the uphill climb a bit difficult, Rabbi. Suppose you sit down some place here and rest for awhile."

This was addressed to the old man who, in spite of his eighty years, was stepping briskly ahead of the others. All the select men of Kasrilevke came to a halt, raised their eyes and looked for a place for the old man to sit down. But before they had a chance to look around and get their bearings, a creature with a red face and white gloves emerged from nowhere, armed from head to foot, and—made straight for them. All the select men felt a chill run down their backs, and all eyes turned to the old man, wondering what he would say. But he didn't utter a word. He just leaned on his old cane and walked on with the same firm step, like a true hero; the others followed him. The armed creature stood petrified, not knowing what to do with them. Should he detain them? There seemed no reason for that; they weren't molesting anybody. Should he let them pass? Surely he couldn't without first ascertaining what sort of people they were. He turned his head around and followed them with his eyes right to the top of the hill. There they stopped and rang the bell at the gate of a luxurious house.

Now it's time we inquired where this delegation from Kasrilevke was going—to whom and for what. They were going to rich men to gather contributions, to ask for bread, to awaken pity for the poor, wretched town of Kasrilevke. For a great misfortune had befallen it. You have known me for many a day now, and you know that I am not one for carrying bad tidings. But how can I help it? It's high time that you knew:

Ladies and gentlemen, Kasrilevke has been burnt out!

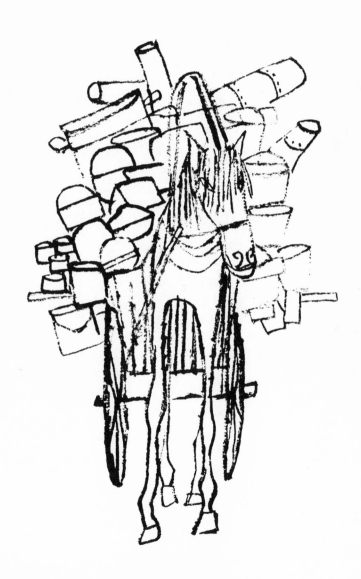

Yes, my friends, Kasrilevke was burnt down. But don't imagine for a minute it was just an ordinary fire.

There have been plenty of fires in Jewish towns and cities this summer—God save the mark. But then there is a difference: there are fires and fires. Kasrilevke, it would seem, wanted to show off to the world. So it said to the other Jewish towns: "Did you say you were on fire? Ha-ha. Just leave it to me and I'll show you how a town can burn."

The long and the short of it is that Kasrilevke caught on fire like matchwood. But no. We shall leave the description of the fire in Kasrilevke to our colleague Fishel the correspondent—that's his job.

On the very next morning after the great fire, Correspondent Fishel (who was burnt out himself and barely escaped with his life) miraculously managed to find pen and ink somewhere, and sent out correspondences to all the Jewish papers, couched in ornate language, written in an unusually beautiful hand and to the following effect:

"A voice is heard in heaven. The daughter of Kas-

rilevke weeps over her great misfortune; she will not
be comforted. An affliction upon an affliction! A
wound upon a wound. Scarcely had Kasrilevke re-
covered from the 'panic' that had been loosed upon
her and which I described in a previous correspondence, when a new burst of wrath descended upon
the hapless town, and Kasrilevke drank to the dregs
the bitter cup out of the hand of God. A
conflagration came down from the heavens and set
on fire the town from one end to the other, consuming it to the ground, with no mercy for the
sacred houses of worship and study. Even children,
infants, ay, sucklings at their mothers' breasts, as-
cended heavenward with the fiery flame. Old folk,
too, poor, ailing and feeble, were food for the fire on
the day when the Lord manifoldly visited His punish-
ment upon us for our grievous sins. Even on His
sacred Torah He had no compassion: it was burnt
along with the old synagogue. We are now under the
canopy of the heavens, forsaken, naked and barefoot,
hungry and thirsty; and with bated breath we look
to our merciful brethren, the sons of the merciful.
We beg of you: Have pity! Let your favor shine
upon us! May compassion be awakened in your kind
hearts and may your willing hands stretch forth aid
to us as soon as possible, for we have become sorely
impoverished. Nourish us and sustain us, and do not

allow the small remnant of Jacob to perish!"

You'd think there would be no harm in printing in a Jewish newspaper this entire heartbreaking correspondence whose every word was a sigh and every letter a tear. But no. They needs had to abbreviate poor Fishel's write-up, squeeze it and extract its essence. So they crowded the following two lines in small type into some obscure corner:

> Kasrilevke has been burnt out, not without loss to human life. Aid is solicited.

To be sure, the newspapers say in their defense that they aren't to blame, seeing that they receive almost daily news items from this same Fishel of Kasrilevke. If they were to print—so they argue—everything that this correspondent writes, they'd have to issue a special edition for the "little folk" of Kasrilevke, involving the maintenance of special presses and a special staff.

Isn't that a wonderful excuse? When anything untoward happens, everyone seems to be fed up with Kasrilevke. Mind you, when the same editors and publishers are about to issue new journals and books, they don't begrudge sending to Kasrilevke their fine and fancy prospectuses, and they aren't too proud to call the little folk "dear and honored subscribers." True, enough, their papers can't boast of a large circulation in Kasrilevke. To be exact, they have all told in the whole of Kasrilevke no more than one subscriber, Zaidl, our old acquaintance Reb Shayes' Zaidl. That's where our Correspondent Fishel gets his news, and after him all the rest who crave for the printed word.

But what's all this got to do with Fishel's correspondences? Why do all his letters and all his writings make straight for the basket under the table even before it is known what they contain? When a Jewish holiday comes round, and the editor reels off a lot of high-flown words about the people of Israel, and in his excitement exclaims:

"Who has counted the dust of Jacob? And who has numbered the horsemen of Israel?"—does he not include the "little folk" as well?

Or take, for example, our critics, those who detail our faults and call us by such high-sounding names as "exploiters," "parasites," "bloodsuckers" and so on—don't they have in mind Kasrilevke too? Kasrilevke may well apply to itself the proverb, "When it comes to carcasses, I, too, am counted with the cattle."

All the same, you mustn't suppose that after the fire the inhabitants of Kasrilevke stopped with Fishel's correspondence. They sent out letters as well —letters written in the grand style and composed by none other than Fishel—to all Jewish communities, wherever there might be a Jewish man of wealth whose name is known in the world. They wrote to Yehupetz, Odessa, Moscow, London, and even to Paris, to the great Rothschild in person.

Lest you be surprised at Kasrilevke going as far afield as Paris and aiming to reach Rothschild, let me explain that for years this town used to receive from him, on the eve of every Passover, the sum of one hundred francs, addressed to Rabbi Yozifl. That was *mo-os chitim* for the purchase of *matzos* for the poor. True enough, for some time Rothschild had stopped sending them *mo-os chitim;* nobody knew why. All the same they continued writing letters to him on every happy occasion as well as—may heaven spare us such misfortune—at every sad occurrence. But then you might wonder why they had had no answer whatever from him in all these years. There may be several explanations. For one thing, maybe he got fed up reading their interminable letters. (As the saying goes, "You can get tired even of eating *kreplech.*") What's more, maybe the address wasn't quite correct. Also, it's possible that something happened to Rothschild in Paris like what happened—if you will pardon the comparison—to Pharaoh, the king of Egypt, as we read in the Scriptures: "Now there arose a new king over Egypt, who knew not Joseph," or pretended he didn't know. I mean Rothschild's secretary, the one who receives the mail and reads all the letters. Those that he likes he shows to his master, the ones he doesn't like—well, down they go, straight into the basket. Mind you, I don't know for certain, but I figure that's how they work things.

Well, as you can see, Kasrilevke is the kind of town that has dealings with, corresponds with, the whole world—for which heaven be praised. And so, as soon as the great calamity happened, word was immediately sent out through Correspondent Fishel; the news was broadcast and relief was awaited for the great misfortune that had befallen the town.

III *Disaster*

How did the misfortune come about? It started in the old bath house. A beam caught on fire on a Thursday; the fire spread to the roof, and before they knew it, the whole bath house was one mass of flames. When "Adam" and "Eve"—the keeper of the baths and his wife (so called because they had to run around nearly naked)—ran out of the building, barely managing to escape with their lives, the first thought that came to them was: "Good Lord—the rabbi!" In the twinkling of an eye "Adam" the bath keeper was in the house and carried the rabbi out in his big strong arms, as if he were a little child; and like a little child, Reb Yozifl the rabbi shielded his eyes against the fire, which lit up the river with its willows and marshes, and a large section of the sky toward which the fire was leaping and the smoke was rolling, heavy smoke shot through with glowing patches and sparks. Everything now looked different, took on a grotesque beauty and a lurid redness. Everything was bathed in red—the river, the sky, the willows, the people. Reb Yozifl had never before seen anything so red and so beautiful; and he just couldn't suppress his fascination. When "Adam" set him down on the ground, he said to himself: "How beautiful and how marvelous is God's world!" But he stopped short and, turning to "Adam" and "Eve," he inquired:

"Children, you aren't hurt, God forbid, are you? Praised be His name, the fire hasn't done you any harm . . ."

"Did you say the fire hasn't done us any harm?"

the keeper of the baths burst out, adding with an ironic laugh: "What has done us harm then, the water?"

"I don't mean that," the rabbi said apologetically. "I am talking about the miracle by which we escaped with our lives, praised be the Creator."

"Our lives? What good are our lives when our bath house is gone?"

"You're talking like a child," Reb Yozifl retorted, shielding his face from the fire with both his hands, "just like a child, that's how you're talking. Where is it written that you must absolutely have a bath house? When you were born, you little goose, were you born with a bath house, by any chance? Or do you expect, in a hundred and twenty years, to come to the other world—God willing—with a bath house? Let me tell you a parable: Once upon a time there was a king . . ."

Reb Yozifl, as was his wont, was about to narrate a very beautiful parable about a king, but the keeper of the baths interrupted him at the very start:

"Never mind the king, just forget the king. Better see, if you please, the way the fire seems to be rolling in that direction, toward the town; and the wind seems to be blowing a bit too hard. I'm afraid it's going to catch Leyvi Mordecai's house and stables. If that happens—then goodbye, Kasrilevke!"

And as though these words had been uttered in an evil hour, the fire did hurl itself at Leyvi Mordecai's house and stables, lighting up a new section of the sky. There was a crashing and crackling noise, mingled with the bleating of goats. A few fowls dashed downhill, wings outstretched and feathers puffed out. Now all the hill, all the town, all the sky were lit up. Strange shouts and echoes came up all the way from the town. The shouting grew louder and louder and was fused with the barking of dogs, the mooing of cows, the screeching of women, the weeping of children, and the cries of "Water! Pails! Help! Hurry! Fire!" Suddenly a mass of flame on four tiny legs was seen leaping downhill toward the river; it executed a dancing movement, shook its horns and made straight for the river. But it didn't get that far, tumbled and fell flat on the ground feet up, shook piteously, and let out a curious bleat in a cracked voice. That was a goat—poor thing—which in its stupidity had leaped into the fire and, straightway regretting what it had done, had leaped out again. But it was too late—her coat had caught on fire and the flame spread. So she started to run helter-skelter, frantically, nowhere in particular, without design or reason.

Nor was there any more design or reason in the way the men and women of Kasrilevke were running about, scurrying from one street to another, like poisoned mice or incompletely slaughtered hens—black with smoke and looking like demons—and telling one another the tidings:

"Do you know? Elye Dovid's place is on fire!"

"Have you heard? It's getting close to the market place!"

"Do you know the latest? The whole town is on fire! Thunderation—the whole town!"

"Burning like a thatched roof! Like a load of hay!"

The fire raged and stormed like a tempestuous sea. The wind carried masses of flame and swirls of sparks. The sparks fell on the old, bone-dry roofs, thatched or shingled. There followed a cracking and rolling, a falling and bursting, a crashing and crackling—merged with screams and echoes, shrill shouts and weeping. Phantoms and demons, rather than humans, scurried hither and thither like mad, dashing in all directions like wounded beasts, while the monstrous, lurid flames lighted up and brought into relief their ghastly, agonized, terror-stricken faces. Kasrilevke was burning, burning like matchwood.

IV *Reb Yozifl Challenges the Creator*

While the bath house was still on fire, neither "Adam" nor "Eve" thought any more of Rabbi Yozifl. But later on, when all that was left of the building were just the iron boiler and the chimney (even the women's bath had burnt down to the ground), "Adam" and "Eve" remembered the rabbi with a start. He wasn't there! They vainly looked for him at the well, the bank of the river, the marshes, and subsequently in town, among the burning buildings.

"Anybody see the rabbi?" the keeper of the baths inquired of the wretched, burnt-out people fleeing from town. They were so bewildered, however, that they hardly heard what was being said to them, and asked in amazement with a terrified look:

"What rabbi? Whose rabbi?"

Where then was Reb Yozifl? When he had collected himself and become aware that the whole town was in danger, he jumped up, snatched his old fur hat and stick that had been rescued from the fire and started out for his former parishioners in the town, without any clear idea of where he was going

and why. Considering his eighty years, this meant
quite a stroll. But when he saw the sea of fire in front
of him, he didn't feel his legs. He was carried along,
as though on wings, toward the old synagogue,
where he had spent nearly all his life in communion
with God. He mused: Was it possible that the Eternal would not work a miracle with His own house?
Was it possible that the Creator would not protect
His Torah, His own Torah? While these thoughts
were running through his mind, Reb Yozifl reached
the old synagogue at the very moment when the fire
was raging all around it. Red tongues were shooting
out from all sides and lighting up the half-collapsed
roof and the peeling yellow walls of the ancient Kasrilevke house of worship. Another minute and God's
house would be wrapped in fire.

Reb Yozifl's mind refused to grasp how Jews
could be standing by. Why weren't they rescuing
the synagogue, the sacred books, the scrolls of the
Law? Instead he saw them running hither and yon
like madmen, leaping into the fire, rescuing sick old
women, little children, chairs, beds, pillows, pots,
household things, and bedding—and God's house
was being forgotten, left to the mercy of the flames.
How could a thing like that happen?

Reb Yozifl tried to shout and call for help: "The
holy place! The synagogue!" No one heard him. In a

minute Reb Yozifl was in the synagogue himself and made straight for the Holy Ark, took out one scroll after another, barely managed to get back to the street alive, deposited them some distance from the door on a broken chair which somebody had hurled out of a house. Standing near the sacred objects, he thus addressed the Creator of the universe in a loud voice:

"I have done what I could. I have saved everything I was able to; I have left the rest of the sacred books to You. I won't budge from here for a moment. Let's see You consume by fire Your own Torah which You gave us through Moses Your servant on Mount Sinai . . ."

Just then the keeper of the baths came along, our friend "Adam." His heart had told him that the old man must be somewhere near the synagogue. Seeing the rabbi standing not far from the burning building, "Adam" didn't dilly-dally very long, picked him up in his brawny arms and carried him, along with the scrolls, away from the fire and down to the burnt-down bath house by the bank of the river.

v *After the Disaster*

It is customary not to pay as much attention to re-
verses during the battle as after. The dead are
counted only after the conflict. When it is all over,
that's the time for adding up losses.

That's how things were done in Kasrilevke too.
Not until the day after the fire did the townsfolk become aware of the enormity of the misfortune. To
start with, people told all kinds of curious tales to
one another: how and when and where they had
found out that there was a fire. It goes without
saying that everybody had his own story, and a long
story at that.

One man told how he had come home yesterday—
can you beat that?—early in the evening, as there
was nothing to do all day, and—can you beat that?—
he got as hungry as a wolf at night and there was
nothing to eat, and—can you beat that?—he went to
bed early, and—can you beat that?—he couldn't fall
asleep because he was hungry, and—can you beat
that?—he did go off to sleep half an hour before the
fire and was sound asleep. Suddenly he heard an
uproar: "Fire! fire! . . ."

Another man told a better story and a longer one, too: how he got up early yesterday, almost before daybreak, and stepped out on the market place, hoping to buy one thing or another, a polecat, a bit of chaff, a bag of potatoes—anything to turn an honest penny. The upshot of it was that there wasn't a living creature there, or to be exact, just one peasant with a bag of coal. So he asked him: "Peasant, how much do you want for your coal?" So he replied: "Fifteen kopecks." So he asked him: "Maybe you'll take ten kopecks." So he said: "Fifteen kopecks." Apparently he had memorized fifteen kopecks and wouldn't let go of the bag for less, not on your life. So the man bought the bag of coal from the peasant, loaded the bag on to his shoulders—and so on and so on. His long-drawn-out story in the end led up to the fire. It all came to this, that when the fire started he was dead to the world; they had all they could do to rouse him.

A third man had a still better story. It went back to the day before yesterday and was interminably long, even longer than the one about the bag of coal. Suddenly a woman butted into the conversation:

"Don't mind his tales, his cock-and-bull stories, let *me* tell you how it all began. On the Thursday, before the fire, I was sieving some flour for Sabbath loaves. Brokhe's husband, Berl, had brought it. What flour!—God save the mark!—May the lives of our enemies be as sweet as it was . . ."

There followed an endless story, a story about bitter flour and bitter yeast and a kneading trough which her neighbor whose name is Pessel—quite an impossible woman—and so on. It was an interminable tale, and it seemed as if she never would get to the fire, not in her lifetime.

These accounts of the fire were punctuated by the tears, the lament, the wailing and the whining of embittered hearts, tortured souls, homeless, wretched, poor, poor people. Here stood a mother, wringing her hands and weeping for her baby which was burnt up, poor thing, along with its cradle; and there a Jew was silently crying over his old sick father who happened to be sleeping in the attic that very night—something he had never done before—and was burnt there to ashes. And here a girl was pounding her head with her hands and screaming: "Mama! Mama! Mama!"

Don't take it amiss, dear reader, if I break off in the middle. My muse which stands over me as I write is, like all the folk of Kasrilevke, a merry soul, poor but merry. She hates tears, and has little use for sad scenes. She says that tears are only what's wet and salty, and that all the other tears which the writer

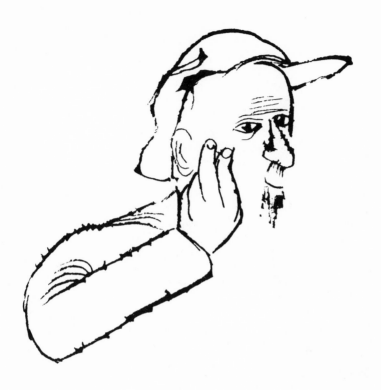

pours out on paper are only dry, affected tears and don't mean anything. It's her opinion that it isn't he who conveys pain that suffers but he whom "it hurts." And so we shall pass over the heartbreaking and gruesome scenes and go right on with our story, stopping only to estimate the damage that the citizens of Kasrilevke suffered from the fire.

The only trouble is, however, that we can't begin to calculate the losses that the town sustained. That's one thing. Secondly, what good will it do to calculate them? Do you suppose that anybody will make them good? The insurance companies, as if acting in concert, have long ago crossed Kasrilevke off the map, as if there had never been such a place in the world. Moreover, who can evaluate another man's possessions anyway, especially after they're gone with the wind and smoke? Household things in general, and especially those in Kasrilevke, have an incalculable value. Old rags and rubbish, shattered looking glasses and chipped crockery are as dear to a poor man (if not dearer) as the most magnificent mirrors and the costliest china are to a rich man. When a rich man loses an object he can buy another one for money; but who can compensate the poor man for what the fire has consumed?

That's how the burnt-out people of Kasrilevke argued. But they realized that they'd get nowhere with arguing and philosophizing; they had to do something about it, think up something, devise a way to save the town. What could they do to prevent the town from being obliterated? It's no trick to have the townsfolk scatter all over the world, going from house to house asking for alms, as burnt-out people frequently do. Surely that was no solution. They had to see to it that Kasrilevke should remain Kasrilevke. That's what they racked their brains about.

To all the stirring and heart-rending letters which were sent out to Jewish communities everywhere, all in all only a few towns responded, themselves as poor as Kasrilevke. Some of them sent in a bit of bread, others some old clothes and still others a few roubles in cash. But this didn't go very far, and the situation began to look alarming. Things soon reached such a pass that people stopped crying, wailing, and even groaning. This is how a man will act when he is on the point of freezing to death: he begins to sink silently into his eternal sleep.

As always in such cases, Reb Yozifl now came to the fore with all the strength which God put into his old feeble body. He convened a meeting of the leading citizens. What's more, he assembled them in person, without the aid of beadles. Nor did he assume a lofty air before them. He simply stood up and addressed the whole audience in these words:

"Listen, my dear children, to what I am going to tell you. It isn't I that's talking, but He who lives eternally is telling you through my sinful lips: Don't worry—your prayer has been granted. I assure you that all will be well, God willing. How so? you might ask. Here is the explanation: true enough, we have been visited with fire; we have been burnt out ourselves and our sacred books have gone up in flames. Human lives have been lost too. Yes, tiny little tots, poor innocent things, have been burnt to death. Of course this is an enormous and dread visitation, which we doubtless deserved at the hands of Him that lives forever. But we mustn't mourn unduly for what's happened. To begin with, our mourning will avail us nothing, and secondly, we shall be proving to Him who lives eternally that we consider the destruction of Kasrilevke to be a worse calamity, heaven forbid, than the destruction of Jerusalem and the destruction of the Temple. Let me illustrate what I mean with a parable. Once upon a time there was a king who had an only son . . ."

Then Reb Yozifl told them a very beautiful parable about a king, as was his habit, concluding with the following words:

"And so you can easily see that it is sinful to complain. We simply must pluck up our courage. Now, my dear children, let us take our sticks in our hands and let us go up and down the land. Do take my advice, children; I'll go along with you. I assure you that no matter where we go, we shall, God willing, find grace in the eyes of our rich brothers, and they won't let us down. Up, fellow Jews, gird your loins and let us go!"

As he spoke, Reb Yozifl straightened out his back, and a light illumined his face. He felt young and vigorous, as if he were still in his prime, a hero ready for battle. The whole audience, too, felt cheered and ready for the expedition. There was just one question to be settled: Whither? Where were they to go to first? There were so many Jewish towns—may no evil eye harm them—and so many rich men.

The question as to who should join the expedition caused quite a commotion in town or, as Fishel put it in one of his correspondences, "stirred it to its depth." There were a lot of people in Kasrilevke eager for this trip. Everybody, almost the whole town, was ready to go. Everyone wanted to have a share in the good deed. Or maybe they just wanted the airing, a chance to stretch their legs. You get musty and stiff staying in one place. Every human being is impelled by some secret temptation; and so there are times when you want to see the world, meet people, and then bring home some news, heaps of news.

As a matter of fact, what can be more pleasant than having people welcome you back from a trip, eagerly crowding around you, and staring into your face? You may wonder why. Surely your face is like all other faces. But then, after all, you *have* just returned from a journey, and that does make a difference! When you talk to your townsmen and tell them what's happened on the road and describe the wonders of the metropolis, hundreds of people

gaze at you, thirstily swallowing your every word.
Your prestige is suddenly raised in everybody's eyes.
You get to be somebody in town, a man, yes, a hero
for at least a few days. True enough, the few days
soon pass and the hero loses his new-won prestige
and reverts back to what he was—just an ordinary
inhabitant of Kasrilevke, like the rest. All the same,
who wouldn't like to be a hero? The hero of one
hour is still a hero!

But coming back to the proposed trip, is it really
possible for a whole town to rise up and set out on a
tour of the world? So it was agreed to select a deputation of a few chosen men. Now the trouble started
all over again: Whom were they to select? It goes
without saying that you pick the rich men and the
most prominent citizens. But you'd be a pretty smart
man to draw the line in Kasrilevke between a rich
man and one who isn't rich, between a prominent citizen and one who isn't a prominent citizen. For you
must bear in mind, when all is said and done, that
every man in town is a prominent citizen; and as for
wealth, well, even the rich men in Kasrilevke are—if
they will pardon me for saying so—not far removed
from poverty. All the same, every town does have its
"aristocracy." Come now! Surely you aren't going to
send the bath house keeper and the water carrier. So
it was decided to delegate the trustees of all the syna-

gogues and of all the societies, along with the old
rabbi, Reb Yozifl—that goes without saying.

So the delegates packed up their bundles, each one
taking along his standbys—prayer shawl and phylacteries and umbrella—and such other necessities.
They engaged two big covered wagons and bade farewell in proper style to the town, which went forth
to see them off and wish them Godspeed. Then the
delegation got under way, praying that the hour
might prove to be a lucky one.

For two days and two nights our chosen ones
jolted in their covered wagons over mud-caked
roads, getting their breath only when they had to
stop at some inn for their prayers, or to get a bite to
eat, or to have the horses fed. Not until the third day
did they arrive at the railway station, feeling bat-
tered, bruised, and worn out.

Here the select men made a dash for the ticket
window, hurling themselves en masse and all but
choking one another. The Jews at the station stepped
aside and said jestingly: "Quiet please—Kasrilevke is
on the march!" You can imagine how respectfully
the Gentiles stopped to contemplate these Jews who
were talking all together, breathlessly and at the top
of their voices, while gesticulating vigorously with
their hands. When the first bell rang, as a signal to go
aboard, an uproar broke out among the select, a veri-

table panic: they jostled one another, ran like mad and raised a terrible racket, punctuated by shouts of: "Laizer! Lozer! Chananye! Michel!" The gendarme looked at the watchman with such an expression that the poor fellow had to hide his pock-marked face with both hands, so as not to be seen laughing with his big mouth wide open and showing his long white teeth. In the end he ejaculated shrilly: *"Yak vorony zlitalisia Zhidy"*—Jews flock together like crows.

The railroad officials were even less impressed by the prominent citizens of Kasrilevke. The conductors shoved them all into one coach, with the common people, and treated them as anything but respected citizens, trustees, deputies traveling on an important mission for the public weal. Here our chosen ones were subjected to all kinds of trouble, anxiety, pain, and embarrassment—such as Jews are accustomed to suffer.

To begin with, they stepped into a coach which, but for the fact that those in it had human faces, our delegates would certainly have taken—if you will excuse the expression—for a pigsty. The mud was so thick, the smoke so blue, and the odor so vile, that our respected citizens of Kasrilevke, although they weren't particularly fussy themselves about such matters, felt such a choking sensation in their throats that they thought they were going to pass out. And the congestion was simply intolerable! They were packed like sardines! And the passengers were such common people, workmen with big, queer-looking and strangely malodorous sacks on their shoulders and even more malodorous bast shoes on their feet. To make matters worse, they were smoking a kind of tobacco that could knock one down. And there was no place to sit. Wherever they went and tried to sit down they were chased away:

"*Pashla von, parkhatye—zanyato!*"

Translated into our vernacular it would amount to this: "Beg pardon, Mr. Jew, this seat is taken." Everything was taken. Even when seats weren't occupied, they were told they were. The select men of Kasrilevke simply had to stand on their feet, huddled together in a corner like sheep, crowding and squeezing one another, all the while talking at the top of their voices as well as with their hands, and all together, as usual.

They were, of course, talking about the railway and modern transportation in general, deriding, simply laughing to scorn the cleverest inventions of the day, and recalling longingly the good old covered wagon. True enough, it wasn't all that could be wished for; still it wasn't as rank as this.

"Fools,"—so our fastidious delegates were saying to one another—"idiots, nitwits thought up a railway! Who wants all this racket and uproar? What an invention!—Ha-ha!"

To think that up there, in high places, thousands of scientists and scholars were sitting doubled up, scribbling away, dashing off drawings, sending out wires, forever racking their brains to devise something new to make transportation better, faster and cheaper and have even got as far as airships and airplanes—to think that they didn't know and didn't even suspect that here, in the railway coach, a group of Kasrilevke citizens, the cream of the town, was criticizing, making sport of, and pulling to pieces all their inventions and achievements, and not in subdued tones or in secret either.

Quiet, please—Kasrilevke is on the march!

VII *Among the Nations*

The select men of Kasrilevke kept lashing away at railways and making fun of all and sundry present-day achievements until they got good and tired.

Then they again started looking around for seats, especially for a seat for the old rabbi, Reb Yozifl, since the poor man was by now quite exhausted from the long trip. At long last they managed to find a place for the rabbi beside one of the Gentile passengers. He was a tough-looking fellow with a red blouse over his trousers and an accordion in his hands. He was a bit tipsy or, to be exact, pretty well fuddled, that is, good and drunk and bleary-eyed. He was in the act of singing a delightful song, which he accompanied with his accordion:

> *Katy's Ma felt life's last breath,*
> *So she made ready for her death,*
> *So she made ready for her death.*
> *The will to part completely filled her—*
> *But could she die?—Not if it killed her!*

And then the same thing all over again, but in a louder tone:

> *Katy's Ma felt life's last breath,*
> *So she made ready for her death,*
> *So she made ready for her death.*
> *The will to part completely filled her—*
> *But could she die?—Not if it killed her!*

And then once more, even louder and faster:

> *Katy's Ma felt life's last breath,*
> *So she made ready for her death . . .*

And so on, without stopping, like a machine.

Well, he was at least a jolly neighbor. But on the other side the Lord wished on the rabbi a creature in a sheepskin coat who was in a huff, a man at odds with all the world, who kept spitting. Every time he spat, it was with such fury as if somebody had enraged him by saying something that he shouldn't have said. It was fortunate that Reb Yozifl didn't notice this, for he was not alive to his surroundings. His thoughts were far away, they were somewhere in the big city, with the bigwigs.

Like all the Jews of Kasrilevke, our Reb Yozifl lived in a world of fantasy, always deep in thought and speculation. Just then his fancy had taken wing and borne him away to the greatest of the bigwigs. He saw in his imagination a great palace with golden appointments. In the seat of honor sat the magnate himself. Seeing the Jewish delegation, he rose, bade them welcome and asked what he could do for them. So he stepped forward himself, Reb Yozifl did, and said to him:

"This is how matters stand, thus and so."

And he read off to him a long list of troubles that the Jews of Kasrilevke had endured, how unfortunate they'd always been and especially so now after the great catastrophe. The magnate listened to the story to the very end. Then he rose, stepped up to a cupboard, took out a good round sum, and asked the rabbi:

"Do you think this will be enough?"

"How is one to tell what's enough?" Reb Yozifl replied.

While these pictures passed through his mind, the rabbi was talking to himself, gesticulating, blinking his eyes and frowning, quite unaware of the people sitting on the opposite bench. There was a variety of types among them, including some red-cheeked females who were busy cracking sunflower seeds. They were all laughing very heartily, while jibing at our Kasrilevke folk to their faces, mimicking the way they were talking, gesticulating, and shaking their earlocks. Most of their banter was aimed at the old rabbi with his curious coat and fur hat.

This laughter and derision was not, however, one-sided, for the men of Kasrilevke on their part gave as good as they got. They ridiculed and laughed up their sleeve at these merry passengers and especially at the tough-looking fellow with the red blouse, the accordion and the pretty song which he did not weary of repeating endlessly:

> Katy's Ma felt life's last breath,
> So she made ready for her death . . .

"I guess the yokel has blessed the wine today," a member of the delegation remarked. Another man followed in the same strain:

"His orbs show it all right."

"That's no mean cup he lapped up," a third man chimed in, in rhyme.

"What a cup! It runneth over . . ." somebody quoted a biblical text, while pretending not to look at the subject of their discourse, but eyeing the ceiling instead.

". . . and overfloweth all its banks all the time of harvest," another man completed the scriptural quotation, all the while scratching the back of his neck under his collar.

"How do you like the melody of his hymn?"

"It must be a hasidic tune."

"And such wise, prayerful words!"

"What depth! What piety! What wisdom! Just fancy, Katy's revered mother pretty nearly breathed her last. Now that's no trifling thing, is it?"

Even Reb Yozifl, who had no use for levity, became curious and asked with a smile:

"What do the queer and outlandish words of this song mean?"

Then somebody explained it to him:

"There was, it would seem, one Katy, that is a person whose name was Katy. And this same Katy had a mother. So this mother got ready to die. But she just couldn't make it."

Reb Yozifl pondered over the meaning but couldn't see any sense to it:

"What do you mean, she got ready to die? Does dying depend on the will of man? Our sages tell us, 'Against thy will thou diest.' "

"What can you expect of 'a people that is likened unto an ass'?" a member of the delegation spoke up, shaking his head and looking down on the gang. His compliment was soon returned by one of the latter who tried to mimic Jews praying. He did so by beating his breast with his fist and saying in a curious singsong:

Tatele, mamele, tatele, mamele!"

The rest of the crowd simply split their sides with laughter.

"They are making fun of us. They are making fun of Jews. They make fun of us everywhere," one of the select men said with a sigh, while nodding to the rabbi. Reb Yozifl looked at that creature's contortions and antics and said:

"He isn't laughing at us, my child. He is making sport of himself, his own self. There is nothing to laugh at as far as we are concerned, my dear; they should weep for us and take example by us, yes, take example: seeing what we were and what has become of us."

Reb Yozifl followed up this remark with a beautiful parable, naturally about a king, and everybody listened to the parable, probably not for the first time. Meanwhile, the fellow with the red blouse and accordion kept lowering his tune, coming down half a note at a time. Apparently he was getting tired of it himself:

> *Katy's Ma felt life's last breath,*
> *So she made ready . . .*
> *The will to part . . .*
> *But could she die? . . .*

"Sholom Aleichem!" a new passenger coming out of nowhere exclaimed. "Where are you men coming from and where are you going to? And why on earth have you gathered here of all places, among this kind? Join us, come to our coach. There at least you'll be among our people, among our own."

VIII *Among Their Own*

Like fish freshly caught in a net and then thrown back into the river—that's how our delegates from Kasrilevke felt when they moved over to the other

coach, among "their own," among Jews. Not that it
was much cleaner or roomier there than in the first
coach. It's quite possible that they were even worse
off in that respect. For over in the other coach a lot
of people were at least sitting on the floor, which
wasn't littered with bundles. A sack and a pair of
boots—that was all most of them had. Whereas here,
in their new quarters, among Jews, there was more
noise and greater congestion; it was simply impossible to move about for the bundles that lay strewn
everywhere.

It's a known fact that every Jew takes along on the
road no fewer than two or three bundles; and
women, in addition to their bundles, also lug pillows
and quilts and a lot of rags. A mountain of rags.
Hence, when traveling, Jews don't look so much like
travelers as like wanderers, emigrants going to some
far-away country where you simply can't get either
pillows or quilts or rags—not at any price. That's
why Jews feel at home everywhere. For no matter
where they go to, they take along their home—for
which God's Name be praised—yes, their "ghetto"
and their "galut." For this reason, too, they look the
same everywhere and at all times; they don't change
so easily. They feel their best only when they are all
together. The non-Jewish world is quite willing to
please them and keeps on telling them: "You like to

be together, don't you?—Well, stick together then."

On stepping into the new coach and seeing that they were among "their own," our select men made themselves quite at home, putting their bundles on top of the other bundles, huddling close to one another on the benches, and asking the other passengers to move over a bit. The minute one of the newcomers had a hold on a seat, there surely was no harm in squeezing his neighbor a little, or for that matter squeezing him out altogether. Weren't they among "their own," among Jews?

But don't let this sort of thing worry you. People don't quarrel or call each other names—heaven forbid—over such trifles. They might, of course, wisecrack or insinuate. Well, what's wrong in that? For example, if somebody steps pretty hard on somebody else's foot, the latter may jump up and say, as it were, quite casually:

"Bless you, mister, that's a pretty firm step you have."

Or suppose somebody were to set a suitcase almost squarely on somebody else's shoulder, then the victim makes a derisive remark about the suitcase rather than its owner, muttering under his breath:

"Well now, I guess your suitcase has always enjoyed good health. It certainly hasn't been losing any weight."

If a man shuts out another man's light, the latter remarks:

"Come to think of it, I am afraid you aren't made of glass."

If two Jews do get into a quarrel about a seat on the train, they certainly don't fight over it; they just banter about it and throw out some broad hints:

"Beg pardon, mister, this is my seat."

"Really, what makes it your seat, I'd like to know?"

"Because I've been sitting here."

"What about it? You didn't stop here over the Sabbath, did you? Or does it say, 'This seat is the property of . . .'?"

The seated passenger doesn't mind going to the trouble of rising and looking for the suggested inscription. The onlookers burst into laughter. The standing passenger gets all the more peeved and comes back at the occupant of the seat:

"Well, I'm not so sure about the contents of your upper story."

"What about those bats in your own belfry?" the seated passenger asks him amid the rising laughter of the bystanders. In the end, however, a compromise is reached. The passengers crowd in a bit, they huddle together just a little closer and make room for the man without a seat. After all, seeing that so many

Jews—may no evil eye harm them—are seated, what's wrong if another one sits down? The two who have just been sparring now just sulk a bit. Then they get busy with their watches: "What time is it by your watch?" Or both of them look out of the window: "Say, you don't happen to know the name of this station by any chance?" After this a conversation ensues about stations and trains and business and—it's smooth sailing. A new passenger boarding the train and seeing the two men takes them either for business partners, or relatives by birth or marriage, or at least for two buddies hailing from the same town.

Let the wise men jest for all they're worth. Let them think up proverbs such as: "Live among Gentiles, die among Jews," "Eat *kugl* with Jews, do business with Gentiles," and similar sayings. I stick to my opinion that Jews, and especially if they come from Kasrilevke, feel much better and much more at home among their own than they do among strangers.

IX *The Man Who Knows His Way Around*

The man who came in out of nowhere and shifted our delegates from their coach over to his own was one of those rare persons that you run into only on the road. The minute you meet one of them, you become chummy and confidential with him, as if you had known him for ever so many years. You have no idea who he is or what sort of man he is. He may very well be a Jewish shopkeeper or, for all you know, a stock broker. But more likely than not he is a tailor who has some pull with the authorities and dabbles at legalizing Jewish residence in prohibited areas.

He is a man of medium stature and in moderate circumstances, dark complexioned and reminiscent of the Armenian type, with a short beard, little, black, restless eyes, and wears his hat shoved back on his head. He is energetic and vivacious; he simply can't sit still: he has to be doing something, going somewhere, or talking with somebody. Most of all talking. When he talks, he is in his element. If there is a Jew in the coach, so much the better. Else, a peasant, a soldier, a noblewoman, a priest—any of them will do. When it comes to the worst, he is content with a stoker, a wheel-greaser, anybody at all, as long as he has the form of a human being.

He is sure to get anybody to talk—unless he is a born mute. For he knows—don't you see?—what to talk about and how to open a conversation with any given man. He'll talk to you about anything you like. It is scarcely an exaggeration to say that there is nothing under the sun that he doesn't know and that there isn't a human being in the world with whom he is not acquainted. It's positively a pleasure to be on the train with such people.

Added to all this, he is a good fellow pure and simple—open and aboveboard and friendly. Even though he has never met you in his life, he'll do anything and go anywhere for you:

"Maybe you'd like me to get a ticket for you in the ticket office?"

"Would you like me to help you pack up your things? I'll be delighted to do it."

Meanwhile he'll peek into your baggage, estimate the value of your suitcase, or your fur coat, or your watch. He'll figure out exactly to the minute what time you'll get home and what the transportation of your baggage will amount to. He'll advise you what route to take, what conveyance to use, and where to get off. While talking to you, he'll hang on to your

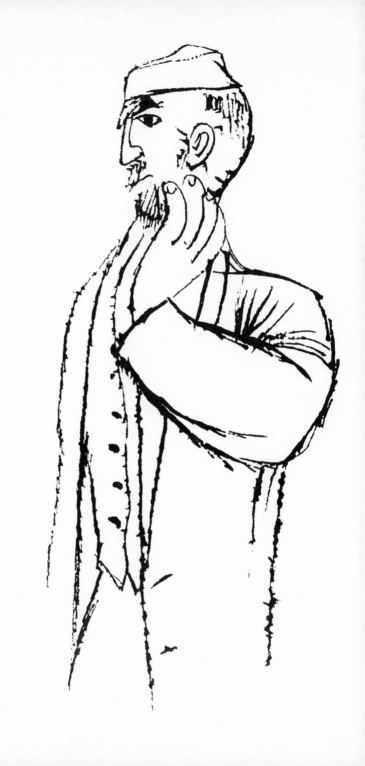

button or drill a hole in your coat with his finger. By now his hat is all but off his head, his cheeks are flushed and his eyes are glowing, as if he were doing something of the greatest urgency. In short, he is the kind of man who "knows his way around."

To our Kasrilevke passengers this man was, so to speak, an oasis in the desert, a heaven-sent blessing, a God-given help. Don't forget the mission on which they had come! Don't forget that this was their first visit to a strange city, and such a big city, too, a city with which they had never had, or ever dreamed of having, the remotest connections. Moreover, they didn't know a soul there.

Our man, too, was delighted with them, positively overjoyed. On learning where and whom they were going to and what it was all about, he showered them with all kinds of advice on their conduct, from the minute they arrived at the station until they picked their way to the place they were making for. The select men of Kasrilevke didn't take their eyes off him, nodded their heads, and hung on every word he uttered.

"You are going, my dear fellow Jews," he insisted, speaking with paternal sincerity, smiling and stroking his little beard, "You are going, my dear fellow Jews, on a very important errand. One might say you're working for a sacred cause. I only hope that you'll

be successful; and that you will be, with God's
help. I'm sure of it, as sure as I am that this is
Tuesday the world over. The important thing is
to know who's who and what's what. The city is
big and covers a large area. It's a Gentile city, don't
you know? But there *are* Jews—may no evil eye
harm them—and rich Jews at that. As a matter of
fact, there are plenty of poor devils too among them,
perhaps more poor devils than rich men. But you
aren't after the poor devils, are you? You say you
have poor devils of your own. I advise you to go
only to the big fellows, the very biggest of them.
Who do you suppose are the very biggest in our
town? You'd like to know, wouldn't you? Well, take
a piece of paper and a pencil, if you don't mind, and
put down their names. I'll give them to you with
their exact addresses and the family background of
each one of them. Don't you see, I know them
through and through. They're all big men, and—if
only they could—they'd like nothing better than to
excel, outdo, and swallow one another, body and
soul. And all of them are straining upward, to a
higher level, imitating the great one, the truly great
one, the lion among the beasts. I can see by your
faces that you know whom I mean. . . . That's his
name all right. 'As his name, so is he.' He is truly a
Lyon. A king—that's what he is, a magnate, a great

magnate, a fabulously rich man, a millionaire. You'd like to know how much he is worth, wouldn't you? Don't ask. No matter what your estimate may be, he's worth twice, three times, ten times as much. For all I know, it's fifty millions. Maybe seventy is a better guess. If you coax me pretty hard, I'll make it all of a hundred millions. He's the man you want to make for last of all, when you're through with all the other big ones. For I take it that you want something substantial, a handful. And if it's a handful you're after, he's your man all right. Let me tell you this: if you happen to strike him at the right moment, there's no telling what he might do. Don't you see, to him a donation of a thousand, or fifty thousand, or a hundred thousand—why, it's like so much small change! Now wait a minute, I've got an idea: here's a still better plan for you."

At this point the man who "knew his way around" fell to thinking. Then he took hold of his little beard and spoke up like a man who has hit on a very happy thought:

"Listen to me, my dear fellow Jews. You tell me that your town has burnt down. If that's the case, you want some lumber to rebuild your houses, don't you? Well, it so happens that he owns a forest not far from your parts. I'm telling you, you've never seen the likes of it—what trees! It means nothing to a millionaire like him to dip his pen in the inkwell and scrawl a few lines to his man: 'Please ship without charge . . .' "

The man who "knew his way around" described with his hand a motion through the air in imitation of the millionaire wielding his pen. On hearing his words, the select men of Kasrilevke started from their places and tears came to their eyes. Now our man, however, brought them down a bit. Apparently he realized that he had raised their expectations too high. So he stroked his little beard, adding:

"But I must repeat to you, my dear fellow Jews, what I have already told you: it all depends on the mood you catch him in. If you happen to run against him when he is in a huff, well, I don't envy you. Don't forget he's a man whose least word is listened to with bated breath, if you know what I mean. He's so important and so influential, what else would you expect? Of course, if you didn't happen to be Jews—well . . ."

At these last words, the select men of Kasrilevke were taken aback. They couldn't figure out what the man was driving at. Just what did he mean, if they didn't happen to be Jews? What else did he expect them to be—hermaphrodites? Seeing that they didn't understand him, the man who "knew his way around" explained himself:

"Don't you see what I mean, my dear fellow Jews? This man is very big, very influential, and highly esteemed by Gentiles. Why, generals visit his house, sit and chat with him, as I'm chatting with you. Well, it goes without saying, when Gentiles are as chummy as all that with a Jew, there's nothing he wouldn't do for them."

I can't say that this explanation was altogether intelligible to our men of Kasrilevke. Their amazement didn't abate. Meanwhile their interlocutor kept stroking his little beard while praising to the skies the bigwigs of Yehupetz. He enumerated for them a long list of "great big men" and "small big men," along with streets and numbers, stopping every now and then to sketch a short but penetrating characterization of almost every one of them. These individual sketches could easily be expanded into a separate book, if our chief interest lay in the personages they described. But since our main concern is the burnt-out people of Kasrilevke, we shall pass over these choice vignettes and return to our delegates from Kasrilevke whom we left at the very start of their sacred mission in the large Gentile city.

x *Chaos*

An *olam hatohu,* a chaos, as described in our sacred books—that's what the metropolis with its bigwigs seemed to our chosen ones of Kasrilevke. The *olam hatohu,* it will be remembered, is a world in which men's souls rove about, penetrating every nook and corner of the globe, seeing and hearing and feeling everything—but they are disembodied souls. Whether because they were so deeply stirred by the stories they had heard on the train from the man who "knew his way around" or because this was their first excursion abroad—one thing is certain: they were not of this world. To put it more precisely, while their souls strayed about among the "big" men, their bodies were far, far away.

Things didn't go well from the first minute on—certainly not the way they had pictured them. To be sure, they went about their business in a prearranged fashion, systematically, following the directions of the man with the small glowing eyes and according to the streets and numbers that he had indicated.

First of all they rang at the doors of the "smaller big men," then at the "greater big men," proceeding ever higher and higher. It would not be stating the case accurately to say that they weren't successful. For they did receive contributions or, as they later boasted in their home town, "a shower of contributions poured down on our heads." Whether such a shower literally poured down, we don't know. One thing, however, is sure, that they had not been in the habit of receiving such donations in their own town and that the sums they were handed in the big city were such as they had seen only in their dreams—and that only rarely.

Such being the case, what then was disconcerting them? Just one thing: they felt that they weren't among their own. They were received like total strangers, like men from a faraway land. They were handed what was their due and were given the hint: "If you don't mind . . ."

Some of the donors wouldn't even look at them and would send out their contribution before the delegates stepped over their thresholds. Others seemed peeved besides and wouldn't let them say a word more than they thought was absolutely necessary. They'd say:

"Burnt out, eh? What's so strange about that? You aren't the only ones . . ."

There were also those who would shout at them and call them all kinds of names: "Fools, burnt-out rats, beggars!" One pale-faced young man, with a pointed nose and a bifurcated little beard, combed right and left, asked to be shown the book.

"What book?"

"The book in which the contributions you receive are recorded."

At this point the old, old rabbi, Reb Yozifl, spoke up:

"The contributions that are given for our fire victims are written in a script and in a language which neither you nor we would be able to read."

Reb Yozifl was, of course, speaking allegorically, veiling the meaning of his words; and despite the sweet smile which never left him, there was a touch of resentment in his voice. He didn't mind so much being suspected of dishonesty. What bothered him was the cold reception they met with everywhere, in every "big" man's house.

In Kasrilevke things were different. There when a Jew gave a donation—even if only a kopeck or, for that matter, a groschen—he gave it with all his heart. For, besides helping a needy man, he was doing a good deed for which there would be a reward hereafter. Reb Yozifl was surprised not to find a single one among the big men to give him an ordinary homely welcome. There wasn't one among them who inquired after Kasrilevke or who cared to listen

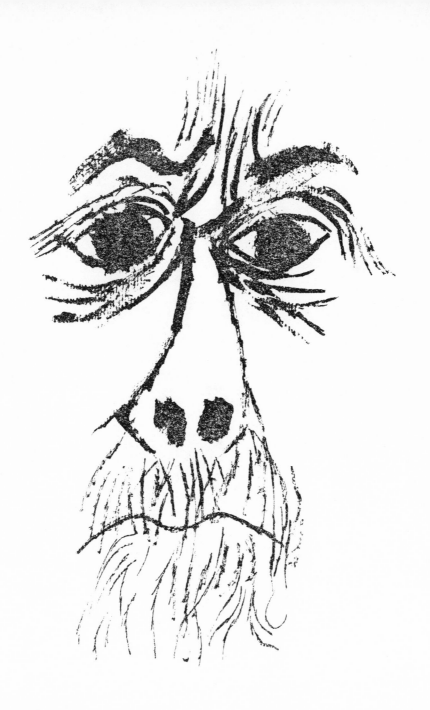

to the story of their misfortune. The minute the delegates tried to talk, go into details, tell about the great calamity that had come upon them, the purse was opened, as if to say: "Take this and away you go."

Always in the habit of condoning everything, Reb Yozifl tried to find some justification for the indifference of these "big men," too.

"These people are living in a world of chaos," he said to himself, as he stepped firmly on and on, not like a man of his age.

It was no longer early when our delegates came up to the house of the very "biggest" of them all, "the lion among the beasts," as the man on the train had called him. Now they remembered the hint that he had given them about this magnate: "If they didn't happen to be Jews—well . . ."

This "well . . . ," added to the coolness which they met with everywhere, in every house, gradually made them lose heart, and now they dreaded to ring the bell of the big man, the very "lion among the beasts." For quite a while they stood by the door and couldn't make up their minds whether to ring in the ordinary way, as they had rung everywhere else, or whether maybe . . .

"Maybe what?"

"Nothing."

"So why do you say 'maybe'?"

"Who on earth is saying 'maybe'?"

"If you aren't saying 'maybe,' so why don't you ring?"

"Where does it say that I have to ring? Why shouldn't you?"

"Did you ever? Looks like an endless story."

"Hush, hush, children, quiet, please," Reb Yozifl called to them, as he pulled the door-bell ever so feebly; his eighty years permitted no greater exertion.

XI *In High Places*

Standing before the door of the very biggest one of them all, the "lion among the beasts," our Kasrilevke delegates had time to indulge in some speculation about the high-born: what were they about just then? What could the "big ones" be doing in their apartments while the "little ones" were standing and waiting at their door, all aflutter about their petty affairs and plans and dreams? Maybe they were poring over their big account-books at the moment, racking their brains, and were so deeply absorbed that they hadn't the faintest idea of what was going on down below. Maybe they were sitting and pondering on new achievements to be attained, or reforms to be instituted in the world with the power of the gold with which the All-Highest had blessed them for the good of their people or that of humanity? And maybe, for all they knew, they were just sitting around doing nothing, enjoying all the pleasures of this world, eating and drinking and sleeping, just like ordinary people.

Our delegates had lots of time to speculate about these things; for no one hastened to open the door at Reb Yozifl's feeble ring. They also had time to exchange their views on the proper presentation of their case to the "greatest of the great," and as to who should be the spokesman. There was no difference of opinion on the latter question; it was a foregone conclusion that that was the rabbi's job. Who else should do it? The real problem was how to broach the subject. For according to the warning of the fellow on the train, you had to know how to handle him and just what to say to him. Did not our sages maintain: "Life and death are in the power of the tongue"? The meaning of this dictum was clear enough: there are times when one word can do more harm than ten thousand words can undo.

The delegates were divided in their opinions; there were two schools of thought, two camps—a right and a left. The right wing was made up of the older members of the delegation who favored the right methods. They argued that the proper way to approach such a magnate was with humble supplication and with a detailed and moving description of the disaster: "There it stood, a town among towns. Suddenly, in the dead of night, a fire came down from the heavens, and the town went up in smoke; Kasrilevke was wiped off the face of the earth . . ." Nor were the gruesome details to be glossed over, so the right wing argued. The magnate was to be told about the sufferings of the naked, barefoot, hungry, and roofless victims, piteously begging for bread. Nor was the narrator to suppress an odd tear or two, or, better still, why not burst into a heart-rending sob?

The left bloc, consisting of course of the younger element, defended the opposite view: "What's the idea of crying, all of a sudden? Are we so many women? Or do you suppose that the rich men are strangers to tears? They have to be won over by the

justice and righteousness of our cause. 'How can such things be allowed?' they should be asked. 'At a time when your streets are littered with gold and your people twiddle their thumbs, our poor folk are dying for a spoonful of soup—human beings, your brothers, your flesh and blood . . .' "

"The idea! Did you ever?" the right-wingers retorted in dismay. "You're going to kill it. That's what youngsters are like, every time!"

Fortunately Reb Yozifl was there. So he quickly pacified them with soft words, as he always did.

"Children," he said to them, "your dispute is all for nothing. For how can a man—alas, a mere mortal —how can a man know what he is going to say? Take Balaam, the wicked man. He had been bribed and was all ready to curse the Jews. Well, did he imagine that the Eternal One would turn his words topsy-turvy? We're going to sway this magnate, God willing, neither with entreaties nor demands, but with a parable. If the Lord will so bid me, I'll tell him a parable about a king whose wrath was kindled against his own servants and who burnt down his own palace . . ."

What a pity! Such a beautiful parable was broken off in the middle for a reason for which neither Reb Yozifl nor the other delegates were to blame. An outsider was the cause of this interruption, the armed creature referred to at the beginning of this story.

Apparently this man in uniform who was posted to watch the street kept a sharp eye on the Kasrilevke delegation. He didn't like their conduct, the way they went from house to house, turned up their heads to look at the numbers, and stopped every little while to talk things over, all together at the top of their voices, gaggling like so many geese. Their last halt and heated argument especially was as much as he could stand. So he made straight for them—this time more resolutely and more briskly.

On seeing the enemy so close and sensing danger, our delegates all but passed out. There was general agreement that the only thing that could save them now was flight. But where to? Retreat meant running into the enemy's arms. So they started ringing at the door, all together, violently, with all their might. That worked; the door really opened, as if by a miracle, and a red-faced, well-fed fellow in a cutaway coat and white gloves appeared. He ran out of the house in a huff, gesticulating, yelling, cursing, and storming, as if he had run into so many savages, robbers, or roughnecks who were about to raid his master's house in broad daylight.

On seeing an open door in front of them, the Kasrilevke "roughnecks" made a dash for it. But the well-fed fellow with the white gloves shoved them back with all his might. Just then the gendarme with the sword came up, gave a loud whistle and another gendarme likewise armed from head to foot appeared out of nowhere.

In vain the select men of Kasrilevke implored the fellow with the white gloves to let them step inside, if only into the vestibule or the kitchen. In vain they raised their eyes to the upper stories, hoping that the All-High would work a miracle (He can if He will), and that the magnate himself or a member of his household, seeing the danger to which these Jews were exposed, would issue an order from his heights that they were not to be touched.

Unfortunately, however, none of the high-born were looking down, and our delegates, the most prominent citizens of Kasrilevke, headed by their rabbi, Reb Yozifl, were led away with great pomp to a place which is rent-free and where no racial and social distinctions exist—one place where Jews, even if they come from Kasrilevke, can stay as long as they like, if only the Lord will grant them length of life.

XII   *The Miracle*

Whoever thinks that there are no more miracles happening nowadays is making a mistake. True enough, they happen seldom now, very seldom, but they do happen. As a proof I cite the case of our Kasrilevke prisoners. The readers may imagine that like all other authors we exaggerate and think up all kinds of cock-and-bull stories. We wish to assure them, however, that our narrative contains nothing but the unadorned truth.

At the very moment when the above-described incident of the Kasrilevke delegates was taking place before the door of the big man, the "lion among the beasts," at the very moment when they stood all atremble gazing at the windows above them, each one wondering in his heart: "From whence shall my help come?"—from God or man?—just then our railroad acquaintance happened to be passing by, the man who "knew his way around."

He was at the time going about his own business, hurrying along in his characteristic manner, with his hat perched on the back of his head, to all appearances deep in thought. Espying his acquaintances

surrounded by uniformed men, he stopped. He at once smelled what was up and was on the point of plunging right into the thick of it, raising a howl and giving those cops the devil. Why in the name of everything were they molesting these innocent people?

Then he thought better of it. Perhaps he shouldn't interfere after all. He knew himself only too well: he was quick-tempered, and there was no telling what he might blurt out. The more he thought of it (it is always best to think before you act), the more convinced he was that it was unwise to act boldly. So he pulled down his hat, took hold of his little beard, closed one eye—a sure sign that his brain was working—made a rightabout turn and retraced his steps as hurriedly as he had come, like a man who has hit on a brilliant idea and is firmly resolved to see the thing through.

Where was he making for?

We don't know, but it's a good guess that he was heading for none other than "the king among the beasts." For that very evening this man's telephone began to work for all it was worth.

At the police station, meanwhile, there was a veritable upheaval. Pens were scratching, ink was flowing, reports were being drawn up, and the prisoners, who were by now resigned to undertake a long forced march home, were suddenly wakened in the middle of the night, removed from their dark cell and ushered into a brightly lit room. They were led into it with such speed, as if they were heaven knows who rather than just "little folk" of Kasrilevke. True enough, they weren't offered chairs, to say nothing of anybody begging their pardon. All the same, no one was heard yelling at them—heaven forbid—or reminding them of their origin. Quite the contrary, the liberation of the Kasrilevke "roughnecks" was carried out calmly and quietly, albeit with feverish haste, very much like the exodus from Egypt. The petty clerks and scribblers at the desks just couldn't get over the fuss that was being made about "these little Jews."

When our prisoners were first told to go upstairs, if they didn't mind, they exchanged glances and silently bid one another farewell. What was awaiting them up there? Heaven only knew. If only—O Creator of the universe!—they'd get off with nothing worse than imprisonment. For what's imprisonment nowadays when hanging is a daily occurrence? Not that they didn't mind being incarcerated. For, it should be borne in mind, every Jew has a wife and children, and when it comes to their wives and children, Jews are—this must be confessed—frightfully egoistic.

With faltering steps and heavy hearts our delegates were brought before those in whose power it was to

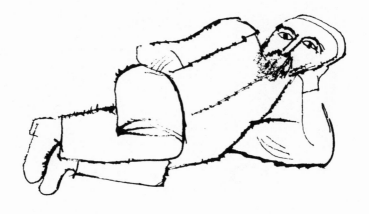

decide their fate. Only one of them walked ahead of the rest with a firm step, as always, though very much stooped and leaning on a stick.

That was old Rabbi Yozifl.

"Who among you is the 'chief rabbi'?" they were asked in a half-serious and half-jeering tone.

"I am," Reb Yozifl spoke up with strange resoluteness and stepped forward bravely, as if he were ready to take sole responsibility for the crime with which the delegates were charged and willing, that very moment, to go to the gallows for them.

The eighty-year-old rabbi appeared glorious, majestically glorious at that moment. His sallow, wrinkled, translucently spiritual face was illumined as if the Divine Presence rested upon it. A youthful fire was kindled in his old eyes; only his hands shook and his shoulders twitched. He waited for what they were going to tell him, ready to listen to anything— no matter how bad—that wicked people might devise. Whom was the old man with eighty years behind him listening to? He actually put one hand behind his back and gazed straight into his interlocutor's eyes with a haughty, almost insolent look, such as the select men of Kasrilevke, frightened to death, had never before seen on his face.

It was a great moment that seemed to drag on and on into an eternity.

"So you are the 'chief rabbi'?" he was asked once

more in the same half-serious, half-jeering tone. "Here, take back the money you've been scooping up for your burnt-out little Jews, and here are your traps and things (evidently meaning their prayer shawls and phylacteries) and those baldaquins of yours (apparently referring to their famous umbrellas)—and away you go, right back home by train. By daybreak I don't want to find a trace of you here. Now beat it!"

On returning home, our select men had many strange and marvelous things to tell about their trip and the ordeals they underwent on behalf of their burnt-out townsmen: how they went and came, what they heard and saw, how the contributions came pouring in—a deluge of contributions (at first it was a "shower," then it grew into a "deluge"), how they were taken prisoner in front of the grand mansion, led to certain "premises," deprived of their "jack," and put in the "cooler." Then came the miracle. The Lord gave proof of what He could do: they were liberated and all their money was returned to them, to the last farthing—and better. For when they were on the point of setting out for home, they were overtaken by a man with a high hat who gave them an additional handout, quite a tidy sum—as a contribution for the burnt-out folk of Kasrilevke, from none other than himself, the man whom that character on the train had named "the lion among the beasts." Well, who is going to question the intervention of the Almighty now?

There's no denying that the delegates from Kasrilevke had plenty to tell; and they haven't told the whole story yet.

Only Reb Yozifl didn't say a thing; he simply didn't let a word escape his lips. He came back from the trip feeling tired, weak, and broken. He wasn't so broken in body as he was in spirit. Then, too, he was preoccupied. He was getting ready, don't you see, for another trip, a trip to a distant land from which no traveler has yet returned. Don't imagine for a minute that Reb Yozifl had nothing to do just because he was a retired rabbi, past eighty, alone in the world, without kith and kin or worldly possessions. For when one is on the point of departing from this sinful world, there is always plenty to do.

EPILOGUE

Reb Yozifl and the Contractor

Everything in the world is progressing and marching onward. So is our town of Kasrilevke.

Kasrilevke has taken a great stride ahead latterly. So much so, that you will be positively surprised if you go there now.

There is one sight in Kasrilevke especially that you will never tire of gazing at. You will see in the heart of the town, where the mud is at its deepest, a massive, yellow brick building—tall and wide—ornamented with iron, with a host of windows, a beautiful, high, carved door, and above it a marble slab bearing the following Hebrew inscription in golden letters:

MOSHAV Z'KENIM

As you look at the building you can't help thinking of a gorgeous velvet patch atop a threadbare lustrine gaberdine, green with age. How comes this luxurious Home for the Aged in the midst of poverty-stricken Kasrilevke? you ask. Was it put up to spite anybody? Or just as a practical joke? Or did somebody make a mistake? Here is the story as it was told to me the last time I was there to visit my parents' grave.

It happened at the time when the railway was being put through Kasrilevke. All kinds of curious creatures came down from Moscow: engineers, surveyors, excavators and such like, and at the head of them all a contractor—a personage of importance and a Jew into the bargain. His name is unknown to this day. Maybe he was one of Poliakov's men, or maybe he was the great financier Poliakov himself, for all anybody knows. But even a child could see that he was worth a fortune—a veritable millionaire. For how else could he afford the luxury of occupying two rooms by himself, gorge himself with chicken, swill wine on weekdays, and dally with the hotel proprietor's young daughter-in-law, the hussy? (She wears no wig even in public and despises her husband, as everybody knows.)

In those days our old friend the rabbi, Reb Yozifl, conceived a plan to erect a *moshav z'kenim* in Kasrilevke—a home for the poor and sick old folk. But why a home for the aged? you might ask. Why not a hospital? There you are again with your questions! Supposing he had set his mind on a hospital; then you'd ask: Why not a home for the aged? I can assure you of one thing, however: he certainly had no personal motive; nothing was further from his mind than the thought of a refuge for his own old age. He simply concluded that a sick old man was to be pitied more than a sick young man. To be sure, an ailing young person was in a bad way too. But if you are ill and old into the bargain, you're simply a burden to the world. Just a loathed dead weight. People despise an infirm old man—there's no gainsaying that.

In short, he made up his mind once for all: Kasrilevke simply must have a *moshav z'kenim*. A home for the aged must take precedence over everything else. And in order to bring home to everybody how necessary it was, Reb Yozifl delivered a sermon in the synagogue on Saturday afternoon, illustrating his talk with a parable: "Once upon a time there was a king who had an only son . . ." But since I am telling you a story, I'd rather not interrupt it with another one. So we'll just defer Reb Yozifl's parable for some other time. I might tell you, however, that although the parable may not have quite fitted the moral in question, nevertheless his audience was completely carried away by it, as they were by all the parables that Reb Yozifl used to tell them. One could only wish that he had been as good at earning his daily bread as he was talented in telling parables.

On hearing his parable, one of the prominent citizens spoke up—one of the most honored, it goes without saying, for who else would dare to contradict a rabbi before a congregation of Jews?

"Yes, indeed, rabbi, there's no denying that you

are right. That was a beautiful parable. The only trouble is: where do we get the cash? A home for the aged costs a lot of money, and Kasrilevke is a town of nothing but indigent, poverty-stricken, penniless, impoverished, destitute starvelings."

"Pshaw! There is a parable that applies to this case too. Once upon a time there was a king who had an only son . . ."

Anyway, the fate of the king and his only son is of no importance. What is important is that on the following day, on a Sunday, our Reb Yozifl in company of two of the most prominent householders, with a kerchief in his hand, set out for the market square and started making the rounds, going from shop to shop and from house to house—the old Kasrilevke method of "raising funds." It goes without saying that no vast fortune can be amassed in this way. Reb Yozifl, however, had plenty of time. He could well afford to wait another week. Rome wasn't built in a day either. It just couldn't be helped: a townful of poor Jews! The only hope were the outsiders—merchants that come down to Kasrilevke, or other transients putting up at the local hotels.

In Kasrilevke, if ever they lay their hands on a bird of passage, they pluck it so bare that it'll warn all and sundry to shun the town: "If ever you have to pass through Kasrilevke, go miles out of your way

to stay clear of it. The town beggars there are simply intolerable!"

On hearing that a Jewish contractor had come down from Moscow, one of Poliakov's men, or maybe Poliakov himself, a multi-millionaire—Reb Yozifl donned his Sabbath best, threw his cloak over it and put his fur hat on his head. Somehow the ceremonial hat didn't go well with the big weekday stick; and he had everybody puzzled. The people argued: it's either one thing or another. If it's the Sabbath, then why a stick; if it's a weekday, why a fur hat? The problem was not solved until Reb Yozifl was seen taking along with him the two most prominent citizens and making straight for the wealthy contractor in the hotel.

I don't know what other Moscow contractors are like. But this contractor who had come to Kasrilevke to put the railway through was a curious sort. Of low stature, limber, with chubby cheeks, fleshy lips, and short arms, he was a frisky little man, running more often than walking, shouting rather than talking and bursting now and then into an explosive little laugh: He-he-he! His little eyes were always moist with tears. All his movements were brisk, hurried, precipitate, and he was dangerously nervous! Not to satisfy his every whim or to irritate him with as much as a single remark was to invite disastrous consequences. His eyes immediately caught fire and he was ready to trample you underfoot or tear you to pieces. He was a very unusual contractor indeed.

He had given instructions at the hotel that no matter who came to see him, no matter who he might be, even if it should be the Governor himself (these were his very words), he was not to be admitted without the proprietor first rapping at his door and being told by the contractor to enter. Only then the proprietor was to report to him who the caller was. Then he would either see him at once or ask him to come the next day.

Needless to say, Kasrilevke had a good laugh at this odd person and his curious ways. Surely only a Moscow contractor could conceive such outlandish notions.

Isn't it enough when a man goes to all the trouble of calling on you—so they argued—must he also stand outside your door and wait till he gets your permission to enter, or else be told to come tomorrow? No, only a Moscow contractor could do a thing like that. There can be little doubt that there isn't a greater man than Reb Yozifl the rabbi, a man of learning and a God-fearing man. Nevertheless his door is open at all times for anybody who may need him. Surely this is an established Jewish custom.

On seeing Reb Yozifl in person and, what's more,

wearing his Sabbath best, the hotel proprietor, a man
with a good-sized paunch, unbuttoned coat and
waistcoat, and a pipe in his mouth, became all flus-
tered:

"I bid you welcome! Welcome indeed! Such a
visitor! Just imagine, the rabbi in person in my
house! Such a privilege! Do be seated, rabbi! What's
that? Oh, you wish to see our guest? With the greatest pleasure!"

The proprietor in his confusion forgot all about the
injunction "no matter who he might be" and "even
if it should be the Governor," put away his pipe,
buttoned his coat, showed the rabbi and the two
most prominent citizens to the guest's door, and himself disappeared.

It is hard to say what the guest was busy doing at
the moment. Perhaps he was in the very act of plan-
ning the railway, figuring where to lay the tracks and
where to put up the station. Or maybe he was lying
down in the adjoining room and dozing. Or maybe,
for all one can tell, he was just sitting there and
having a chat with the proprietor's young daughter-
in-law, the hussy, who wears no wig and despises her
husband, as everybody knows. Who is to say what a
Jewish contractor from Moscow, a personage of importance and a Jew into the bargain, might be doing
—a lone man occupying two rooms? In any event,

when the deputation stepped into the first room, he wasn't there. The door to the adjoining room was open and there wasn't a sound. They didn't want to step any farther. That would be bad manners; he might be sleeping. So they had a brilliant idea: the three of them gave a cough (that's a Kasrilevke custom). Hearing the noise, the contractor bolted out of his room more dead than alive. When he saw the strangers, he flared up and burst out in the true Moscow manner:

"Who are you? What do you want, you so-and-so and so-and-so? Who let you in? Haven't I told them time and again to admit no one unannounced?"

Some say that he used the word *zhidy*, kikes, although it's hard to believe that a Jew would do that. All the same, when a man's wrath is kindled, and especially a millionaire's, there's no telling what he might do.

Our readers who are acquainted with the rabbi of Kasrilevke know full well what a humble man Reb Yozifl was. Why, he'd never dream of being forward. He always preferred to be last. For it was his idea that mortal man must not be in too great a hurry; he has nothing to lose and will never miss anything. But this time he had to step forward, because those "most prominent citizens" were plainly frightened by the millionaire, who was wildly waving his hands at them and emphasizing his fury by stamping his feet. Who could say who he was? Maybe he was one of Poliakov's men, and maybe even Poliakov himself. Such being the case, they naturally had to recede a bit, get a little closer to the door. For there was no telling what might happen. Only Reb Yozifl didn't get frightened this time. He argued this way. It's one of two things: he is either a *big* man or a *little* man. If he is a big man, I don't need to be afraid of him; if he is a little man, there surely can be no occasion for fear. So he spoke right up to him in these words:

"Pardon me, you are shouting at us. Maybe you are right. Forgive us for disturbing you. But we are engaged in the performance of a good deed, and the messengers of a good deed—so our sages tell us—can suffer no injury. You see, we are collecting contributions for a great cause, a home for the aged."

The Moscow contractor stood speechless. The intrusion of the three men into his room, unannounced, like a bolt from the blue, and the conduct of this old man (the fellow with the fur hat) which struck him as both foolish and impudent, so enraged our Muscovite, so infuriated him, that he felt a tickling sensation in his nose, a sense of pressure against his brain, and all his blood rushed to his face. He was simply frantic and so completely lost control of himself that he just didn't know what he was doing. His hand

was raised, as if against his own will, he swung it with all his might and dealt the old man a resounding, flaming slap.

"Take this! This is for your old folks' home!"

The slap sent the old man's fur hat and skullcap flying off his head together, and for a moment the rabbi of Kasrilevke stood with uncovered head—perhaps for the first time in his life. But this lasted no more than a second. Reb Yozifl quickly bent down, snatched up the fur hat and covered his bared head. Then he cautiously felt his cheek and looked at his hand to see if there was any blood. At the same time he said to the guest, speaking softly, sweetly, and with a curious smile on his deathly pale face:

"That's that. I take it that this was meant for me. Now, my dear man, what are you going to give for the sick old folk—I mean the home for the aged?"

What happened next can't be told. No one knows, for "the most prominent citizens," on hearing the language of Moscow from the lips of the contractor, had beaten a hasty retreat. And Reb Yozifl just wouldn't talk about the affair. This is known, however: on leaving the hotel, the old rabbi's face beamed strangely. One of his cheeks—the left— beamed even more than the other. He said with a sweet smile:

"*Mazl tov*, congratulations, fellow Jews, I have

good news for you: we are going to have now, with the aid of the Almighty, a home for the aged—a home that will be a delight to God and man."

The "little folk" might have had some doubts about the rabbi's statement, if they hadn't heard with their own ears the contractor himself say, while tapping his shirt-front with his pudgy fingers:

"Men, I'm putting up a home for the aged in your town. I, I . . ."

Not only did they hear this with their own ears, but they soon saw with their own eyes the contractor walking about the town with the rabbi, then stopping to measure a plot with his stick and saying:

"This is where the building is going to stand; it'll have this frontage and this depth . . ."

Before they knew it, loads of brick, lumber, and other building materials arrived. The structure was under way.

To be sure, there were the curious who tried to question the rabbi, sound him out, get him to talk:

"Rabbi, just what did happen? Just how did this man make it up to you for his harsh words? . . . What did *you* say to *him* and what did he answer *you?* . . ."

Reb Yozifl, however, took no notice of what was said and avoided the subject, merely saying with his ever sweet smile:

"All the same, we are going to have a home for the

aged, God-willing. I'm telling you, it will be a delight to God and man."

Too bad—the home for the aged is unoccupied to this day. Reb Yozifl departed from this world long ago—there is no money to run the institution with.

This has ever been the fate of the little folk of Kasrilevke: when they dream of good things to eat—they haven't a spoon; when they have a spoon—they don't dream of good things to eat.